To everyone I've ever known
    who's had a bugbear of their own.
From queue-jumpers to summer rain,
    to standing-room only on the train. ~ PH

To Angel, for being there ~ CS

LITTLE TIGER PRESS LTD,
an imprint of the Little Tiger Group,
1 Coda Studios
189 Munster Road
London SW6 6AW
www.littletiger.co.uk

First published in Great Britain 2017
This edition published 2018

Text by Patricia Hegarty
Text copyright © Little Tiger Press 2017
Illustrations copyright © Carmen Saldaña 2017
Carmen Saldaña has asserted her right to be identified
as the illustrator of this work under the Copyright,
Designs and Patents Act, 1988
A CIP catalogue record for this book
is available from the British Library
All rights reserved

ISBN 978-1-84869-452-1
Printed in China
LTP/1400/1933/0517
10 9 8 7 6 5 4 3 2 1

BUG
BEAR

Patricia Hegarty   Carmen Saldaña

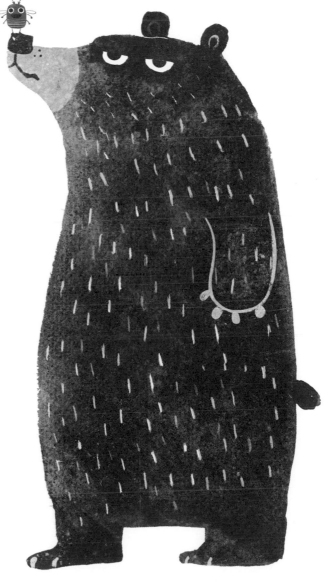

LITTLE TIGER
LONDON

DOWN in the FOREST,
as BEAR had a doze,
A SMALL STRIPY bug
came and sat on his nose.

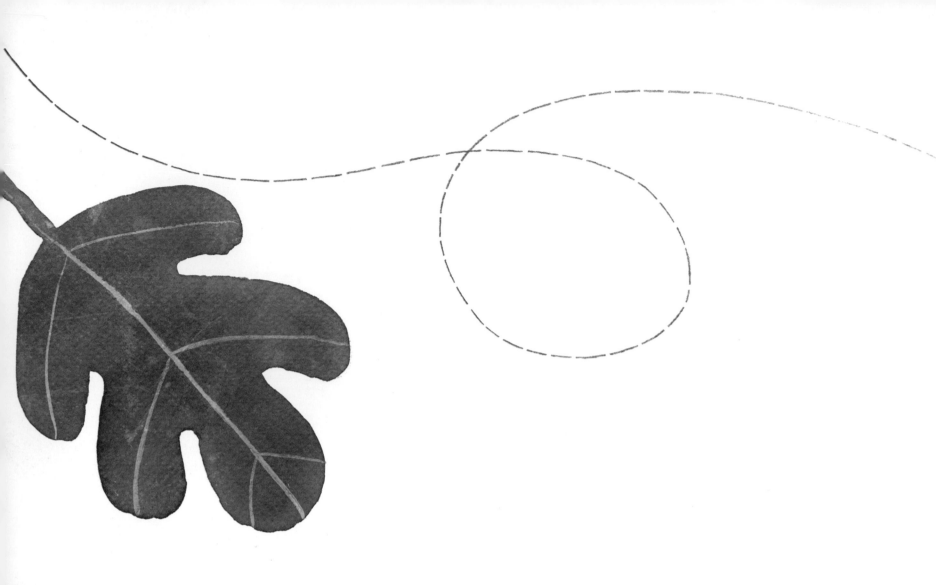

"Good day to you, Bear, I'm just passing through,
Looking for lodgings...
            and I've chosen **YOU!**"

Bear lifted his head and opened one eye,
Then closed it again with a world-weary sigh.

But Bug wasn't easy
for Bear to ignore.

He whirred
and he buzzed

and then buzzed
a bit more.

"You're lovely and squidgy,
and cuddly, dear Bear —
And you DO have a lot
of that warm fur to spare."

"Not Listening! Not Listening! Don't care what you say! My fur's not your home, now PLEASE go away!"

"But your fur is so fuzzy, so soft and so snug –
It's just perfect bedding for a little old bug!"

Bug looped the loop,
then he sat on Bear's snout.
"Come now, my friend, let's both hug it out."

"I don't want to hug you, you fluttering pest.
Why can't you see that I'm trying to **Rest!**"

"You're SO funny, Bear," said Bug with a giggle. And he nestled right down with a jiggly wiggle.

"Stop tickling me, Bug!" said Bear with a snuffle.
"Oh, WHY are you causing this great big kerfuffle?"

Bear hopped and he clopped
and jumped up and down.

He swished and he swatted
then said with a frown...

"Oh, troublesome bug,
why on earth pick on me,
And not one of these other fine
creatures you see?"

"But it's YOU that I like, though I have to declare,
You DO seem a TEENSY bit grumpy, old Bear..."

"GRUMPY?!" said Bear.
"GRUMPY, you say?!"

"I'll give you grumpy –
you've ruined my day!"

"Won't SOMEBODY
help me?"
cRied BeaR with a howl.

"CaN I be of seRvice?"
called cleveR old Owl.

"Oh Owl," whimpeRed BeaR, "please tell him fRom me,
He's GOT to buzz off and just let me be!"

"Don't worry," said Owl, "for I have a PLAN.
Bear can't be your bed, but I know who can.
My friend is just perfect, I'm sure you'll agree.
He's soft and he's hanging
up there in that tree."

"Well, why on eart[h]
I'm all ears," sai[d]

"Alright," said Ow[l]
Now please sa[y]

dn't you say so before?

ug. "You must tell me more!"

on't get in a froth.

ello to my furry friend Sloth."

"I'd be MOST grateful," said Sloth with a grin,
"To have a small bug make his home on my skin.
I don't get about much, because I'm so slow.
Now YOU'LL be my best friend wherever I go!"

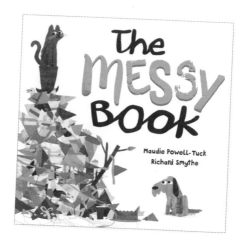

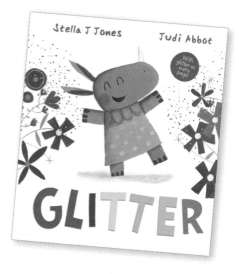

Get the book bug with Little Tiger Press!

For information regarding any of the above titles or for
our catalogue, please contact us:
Little Tiger Press, 1 Coda Studios,
189 Munster Road, London SW6 6AW
• Tel: 020 7385 6333
• E-mail: contact@littletiger.co.uk
• www.littletiger.co.uk

Contents

Teacher's Introduction

Jesus is an exploration of the teaching and life of Jesus Christ in the Synoptic Gospels. This is studied in the light of contemporary Christian beliefs and traditions. Examples have been drawn from different denominations and cultures, as far as possible.

It is important for pupils to understand the effect of Jesus on the moral behaviour, attitudes and lifestyles of Christians. Emphasis is therefore placed on stories of Christians today, or in the past, as living embodiments of the beliefs and values being studied. This makes abstract truths live and breathe with the pulse of modern life. An important dimension to the study of Christian belief about Jesus is the belief in the resurrection and his on-going influence. Christians feel that they are impacted by Jesus today. To study inspired individuals gives insight into the Founder of their faith.

One theologian wrote:

> *We tell stories about God because they permit us to gain some sense of God's intervention in human affairs …The history of an exemplary Christian recollects the life of a specific woman or man, and yet it also expresses the enacted narrative of Christ abiding with the human community, hereby picking up where the Gospels leave off.* (Story-Shaped Christology, *Robert A. Krieg*)

Pupil Introduction

- A study of the Gospels of Matthew, Mark and Luke, investigating the life and teaching of Jesus, and the evidence for his existence.
- A look, too, at some of the people who follow him today and are inspired by his teaching.

1

Searching for Jesus

- Jesus Bar Joseph factsheet
- What is a Gospel?
- Dating the Gospels
- The Synoptics and how they were composed
- The Ingredients of a Gospel
- Ancient copies of books and Gospels
- Ancient writers mentioning Jesus

- Archaeology
- What did Jesus look like?
- Are the Gospels trustworthy?
- The Gospels today in worship, prayer and discussion
- People affected by the Gospels – Bruce Kent, Corrie Ten Boom, Cliff Richard and Kris Akabusi.

JERUSALEM INFORMATION SERVICE

- **Name**: Jesus Bar Joseph
- **Address**: Mary's carpenter's shop, Nazareth
- **Age**: about 33
- **Distinguishing features**: Well built. Dark hair, beard, eyes that seem to look right into you.
- **Occupation**: Presently a wandering preacher with 12 disciples. Used to be a builder/carpenter.
- **Comments**: This man could be trouble. He talks about the coming Kingdom of God – the authorities do not like talk about a new order. Some say he claims to be the Messiah – very dangerous! The Romans are watching him carefully. Others say that he claims to be God – either they are lying, or he is mentally unstable, or we might be hearing more of him in future!

How do we Know Anything About Jesus?

The Gospels

This is a fourth-century manuscript of the Gospels called the *Codex Sinaiticus*. It is in Greek, as the Gospels were originally written in Greek.

Most of our information comes from the four Gospels in the New Testament. The word 'Gospel' means 'Good News', based upon a Greek word, *evangelion*. The four writers of the Gospels are therefore known as evangelists. We do not know exactly who wrote Matthew, Mark, Luke or John. The titles of the books were added later, and it is difficult to tell from clues within the Gospels. Neither do we know how early they were written. Most scholars tend to make an educated guess at the following:

▶ **Matthew** *c.*75–95 CE – Contains some material from Matthew, possibly sayings of Jesus, or Old Testament prophecies he fulfilled.

▶ **Mark** *c.*65–75 CE – Probably earliest Gospel. Mark knew Peter.

▶ **Luke** *c.*75–95 CE – Author might have been a travelling companion of Paul, mentioned in Acts 16:10.

▶ **John** *c.*90–100 CE – A very different style. Could be based upon some material from the apostle John. Thought to be mainly work of a later Christian.

Some have argued that the Gospels were all written much earlier, before 70CE. One reason they give is that there is no reference to the Jewish Temple in Jerusalem having been destroyed by the Romans, in 70CE.

An early Christian writer, Papias, mentions that Mark was Peter's interpreter at Rome, and that he wrote down his memoirs. The early Church met in the home of a woman with a son called Mark, and the Gospel mentions a story about a young man running away when Jesus was arrested – a reference to Mark perhaps?

Mark's Gospel is the shortest, and so many think it was the first. Matthew and Luke also use much of Mark's material in their own Gospels, almost word for word. This suggests that they knew of Mark before they wrote their books, or that they used a common tradition. A few have argued that Mark was written later to simplify the material.

The Synoptic Gospels

Matthew, Mark and Luke are known as the Synoptic Gospels, because they tell the same basic story, with the same order of events. (Synoptic is from the Greek meaning 'to see in the same manner'.) John, sometimes known as the 'Fourth Gospel', tells the story of Jesus in a slightly different order. The cleansing of the Temple, for example, comes at the start of the Gospel rather than near the end, as in the others. Jesus also uses long speeches, whereas he tends to speak in short sentences in the others.

Each Gospel presents a different portrait of Jesus.

▶ **Matthew** – The Messiah, God's promised man.

▶ **Mark** – The Son of God, working wonders.

▶ **Luke** – The Son of Man, healer and Saviour.

▶ **John** – God living as a man.

These do not necessarily contradict one another, they just emphasise different aspects of Jesus.

How the Gospels Were Written

The Synoptics obviously influenced one another. We do not know for sure what was written first, or whether Matthew was written before Luke. Did Luke use Matthew, or vice versa? Scholars have dissected the Gospels and found blocks of material, as below;

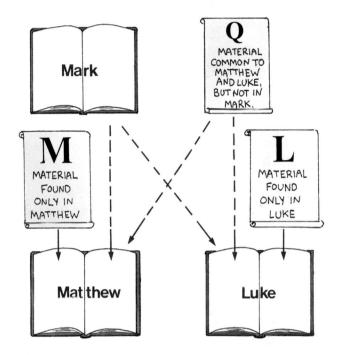

Luke and Matthew used Mark. Matthew and Luke both have extra material in common, nicknamed 'Q', from the German *quelle*, for 'source'. They also have some material that is only in each of their Gospels, and this is labelled 'M' and 'L'. How much of Q, M and L was ever written down before the final versions of the Gospels we will never know. There were probably many traditions circulating about Jesus, many oral, some written, before the Gospels were put together.

The Jewish society of the time was used to passing on information by word of mouth, an oral tradition. People were more disciplined about this than we are now. They had fewer books or scrolls, and fewer people could read and write. Rabbis trained their pupils to remember everything they were taught. One said, 'A well trained pupil is like a well-plastered cistern that loses not a drop.'

An essay is written by taking information from various sources, and putting it into your own words. The Gospels were formed like this, too.

Different Ingredients

A Gospel is made up of many different types of writing.

Some of these types of writing are collected together in sections in the Gospels. There are lists of sayings, parable after parable, healing after healing. The Gospel writers might have collected these stories from various sources, and put them together, not being certain when Jesus said or did them, exactly.

The largest sections in the Gospels are concerned with the last week of Jesus' life, from his return to Jerusalem at Passover time, to his death on the cross, and the events afterwards. Of the 16 chapters in Mark, six are concerned with the last week! The death of Jesus was obviously re-told, in words and maybe in writing, very early on. It was very important for the early Christians. They probably told some of it when they worshipped, especially when they had the bread and wine to remember Jesus' death. Scholars call this section the Passion Narrative. The Passion refers to the pain and suffering Jesus went through.

Parables – stories with a moral

Sayings about how to live

Stories of healing

Prophecies that Jesus was supposed to fulfil

Modern Christians celebrating Communion at the Greenbelt Festival. First of all, the leader gives thanks for Jesus dying on the cross, and then he repeats Jesus' words over the bread and wine. 'This is my body, which is given for you. Do this in memory of me.' (Luke 22:19) and 'this is my blood which seals God's covenant, my blood poured out for many for the forgiveness of sins.' (Matthew 26:28)

Activities

Key Elements

1 What is the meaning of 'Gospel'?

2 Why do some people think the Gospels were written earlier than 70CE?

3 Which Gospel was probably the earliest to be written? Why do people think this was so?

4 Check out some of the clues about the writers. Look up Mark 14:51–2 and Acts 12:12, and v 25. Then look up Matthew 9:9–13, and compare this with Mark 2:13–17.

5 Why are Matthew, Mark and Luke called the Synoptics?

6 a) What different ideas about Jesus are given in each Gospel?
b) Read the following passages and say what ideas about Jesus are present:

Matthew 1:22–3; 5:17; Mark 1:1, 27–8; Luke 4:16–19; 9:18–22; John 1:14.

7 What is meant by Q, M and L?

8 What is meant by oral tradition?

9 What is a parable?

10 What is meant by the Passion Narrative?

11 Match up these references with the types of writing listed:

Mark 2:1–12; Mark 4:30–4; Matthew 5:1–12; Mark 15:21–32.

Parable; Passion Narrative; Healing; Teaching.

12 Test yourself... See if you can draw the diagram about the Synoptic Gospels from memory. Keep trying until you get it right!

Think About It

13 Do you think it matters how early or late a Gospel was written?

14 John contains long speeches by Jesus, but their ideas are similar to shorter sayings in the Gospels. Compare John 3:1–8 with Matthew 18:1–4.

15 Read through Mark, at one sitting if possible. Make a note of any questions or reactions that you have. Have a brainstorming session in class to discuss these.

16 Why would oral reports be more reliable in the past, than today? What do you think the rabbi meant when he spoke about 'well-plastered cisterns'?

Assignment

17 Write four descriptions of yourself, as you would expect from your parents, teacher, friend, and a neighbour. Then think about how alike or different they are.

Ancient Copies

IF THE GOSPELS WERE WRITTEN 2,000 YEARS AGO, THEN HOW DO WE KNOW THEY'RE STILL THE SAME ?

This is a good question. Surely, monks might have changed the text as they copied them over the ages? The fact is that we possess a large number of old copies of the Gospels. The earliest goes back to the fourth century CE, and there are scraps and fragments much earlier than that. The earliest fragment is part of John, kept in the Rylands Library in Manchester. This was found in Egypt, and is dated c.110–130CE. It contains part of the text from John 18:31–3 and 37–8.

It is remarkable how the small portion of text is exactly the same as the modern Gospel, suggesting that there had been no major changes.

Some ancient copies were found by accident, and rescued from destruction. One complete copy of the Bible, dating from the fourth century CE, was found by Count Tischendorf in the monastery of St Catherine on Mount Sinai, in 1859. He rescued this from papers being burnt by the monks! This was acquired by the Tsar of Russia, and later bought by the British Museum.

It is striking to compare the amount of copies of the Bible, and how far they go back, with the work of an ancient writer such as Julius Caesar:

Caesar –*The Gallic Wars*
Written – c.54–45BCE
Earliest copy – ninth century CE
Number of copies in existence – one.

Or, compare the works of the Roman historian, Tacitus:

Tacitus – *The Annals*
Written – c.112CE
Earliest copy – ninth century CE
Number of copies – ten in full, two in part.

Julius Caesar.

Fact Box

Tactitus was a loyal Roman, suspicious of the Christians. Yet, he wrote of Christ as a teacher who was crucified by Pilate, when Tiberius was Emperor. This fits in with the New Testament. Did Tactitus use old police reports from Pilate for his information? Josephus praised Jesus as a wise man, and also agrees that Pilate had him crucified.

Ancient Writers

CORNELIUS TACITUS, ROMAN HISTORIAN. WROTE *THE ANNALS C.*112CE.

In his section on the Emperor Nero, he mentions the Christians. They followed...

CHRISTUS, FROM WHOM THEIR NAME IS DERIVED, WAS EXECUTED AT THE HANDS OF THE PROCURATOR, PONTIUS PILATE, IN THE REIGN OF TIBERIUS.

FLAVIUS JOSEPHUS, A JEW WHO WROTE ABOUT HIS PEOPLE FOR THE ROMANS AT THE END OF THE FIRST CENTURY CE.

AT THIS TIME THERE WAS A WISE MAN WHO WAS CALLED JESUS... PILATE CONDEMNED HIM TO BE CRUCIFIED AND THOSE WHO HAD BECOME HIS DISCIPLES DID NOT ABANDON HIS DISCIPLESHIP. THEY REPORTED THAT HE HAD APPEARED TO THEM THREE DAYS AFTER HIS CRUCIFIXION AND THAT HE WAS ALIVE.

Question

* What solid evidence about Jesus do these writers give us?

Archaeology

Archaeology reveals things about the past by finding objects and ruins under the ground. The material found is usually fragmentary, and it is like working with a few pieces of a jigsaw puzzle. Next to nothing is left behind by individuals from the past, even outstanding ones. There might be a picture here, a scrap of paper there, an inscription on a stone... Jesus, in his day, was not a ruler, or world famous. He was just a wandering preacher. There were no pictures painted, or sculptures made, during his lifetime.

Archaeology has found inscriptions and ruins that tally with various things described in the Gospels, though.

Pilate's Inscription

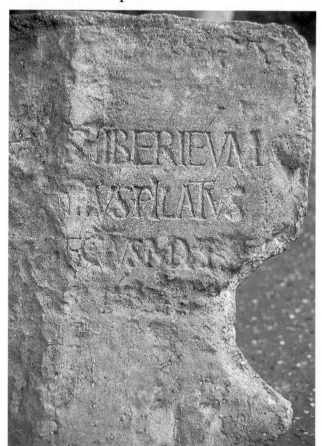

This stone was found in an old, ruined theatre in Caesarea in 1961. It bears the name 'Pilate'. You should just be able to make out the Latin *Pilatus*. Pontius Pilate was the governor of Judaea from 26–36CE, during Jesus' ministry.

The Pavement

These paving stones were found in the crypt of the Sion convent, Jerusalem. These were part of the pavement (*Gabbatha* in Hebrew) where Jesus was tried by Pilate (see John 19:13).

The markings are games played by Roman soldiers scratched into the stone.

The Nazareth Decree

This is a stone found in 1930, near Nazareth, and is now in Paris. A picture of it can be seen on p. 9.

The text reads:

> *Ordinance of Caesar. It is my pleasure that graves and tombs remain undisturbed in perpetuity for those who have made them for the cult of their ancestors, or children, or members of their house. If, however, any man lay information that another has either demolished them, or has in any other way extracted the buried, or has maliciously transferred them to other places in order to wrong them, or has displaced the sealing or other stones against such a one I order that a trial be instituted, as in respect of the gods... Let it be absolutely forbidden for anyone*

Inscriptions Using the Name 'Jesus'

Jesus help

Jesus let him arise

These two tomb inscriptions were discovered in 1945 by a Jewish Professor. They read, 'Jesus, help!' and 'Jesus, let him rise!' These were on Christian tombs, between 40–50CE, showing that prayers were offered to Jesus as God only several years after his death.

Details From Everyday Life

Mark 14:3–9 tells the story of the woman breaking a bottle of perfume over Jesus to honour him. Small, long-necked bottles have been found that could be broken without fragments spoiling the perfume.

Nazareth is described, in the Gospels, as a small town famous for nothing, and only 23 first-century tombs have been found there, confirming its reputation as an insignificant place (see John 1:46).

The Nazareth Decree.

to disturb them. In the case of contravention I desire that the offender be sentenced to capital puniushment on charge of violation of sepulchre.

Just an old decree about grave robbers? This dates from the first century CE, and possibly as early as Pilate's time. Some wonder if the story told by the authorities about the body of Jesus led to this decree being issued (see Matthew 28:11–15).

Activities

Key Elements

1 a) What is the Ryland's Fragment?
   b) How old is this?
   c) Why does it suggest that the text of the Gospels was not changed in any major way?

2 How far back can we trace a complete copy of the Bible?

3 Why should we not expect much information from archaeology about Jesus?

4 How has archaeology proved that Pilate was governor of Judaea?

5 What is the Nazareth Decree and the *Gabbatha*?

6 Why is the Nazareth Decree significant?

Think About It

7 What do you think comparing copies of the Bible with those of Julius Caesar and Tacitus suggests ?

8 If the New Testament text is accurate, must everything have happened as it says it did? What do you think?

What did Jesus Look Like?

We cannot be certain. No description is given in the Gospels at all. He was a Galilean Jew, and therefore his hair would have been dark, and his skin tanned. He was a builder, carpenter or joiner. (The Greek word, *ho tekton*, can mean any of these trades.) This suggests that he was fairly muscular and strong – but he could have been small, we do not know!

It was the custom for some to grow their hair long, including ringlets at the temples, and to keep a beard as a sign of dedication to God.

There is a curious tradition among some early Christian writers which says that Jesus was an ugly man. Many Christians read one of Isaiah's prophecies as relating to Jesus – it is about a servant of God who suffers for the people. In Isaiah 53:2, it says:

> *He had no dignity or beauty to make us take notice of him. There was nothing attractive about him, nothing that would draw us to him.*

The earliest catacomb painting of Jesus.

People from different cultures have their own views of the way Jesus looked.

Perhaps this suggests that Jesus was plain and ugly, though other Christians feel the passage refers to the tortured face of the servant, i.e. Jesus on the way to the cross.

Different cultures picture Jesus as one of their race, though he was a Jew, in fact.

An Orthodox Jew. Jesus was a Jew, he may have looked something like this though dressed in a first-century manner.

> *Discuss*
>
> * How have you always imagined Jesus to look?
> * Do you think it matters what he looked like? Are you upset to think he might have been an ugly man?

Can we Trust the Gospel Accounts?

Ancient writings and archaeology show that the people and places mentioned in the Gospels are real. Jesus was a preacher who was crucifed by Pilate. There are many ancient copies of the Gospels, showing that copyists did not alter things along the way. Yet, can the original Gospel writers be trusted?

No one can prove that they were right or wrong, as such, but there are many indications that the writings are basically reliable.

Aramaic Rimes

Scholars have found that the sayings of Jesus, when translated back into Aramaic, form little poems, and rimes. This is the usual way an Aramaic speaker would have taught, suggesting that these sayings were either truly spoken by Jesus, or were written into the Gospels, very early on, by people who shared that culture.

Oral Tradition

We have already seen how seriously people memorised teaching and passed it on. Rabbis trained their disciples to remember their teaching in fine detail.

Eyewitnesses

If the Gospels were written before 70CE, then numerous eyewitnesses of the events they describe would have still been alive. Even if they were written later, some would still have been alive, especially when Mark was written. It is interesting that an early Christian, Papias, said that Mark wrote Peter's memoirs.

Miracles?

The miracles of Jesus make the Gospels hard to believe for some – surely there has been exaggeration? Ideas about miracles will be discussed later, but suffice to say here that the miracle stories were present in the earliest traditions in the Gospels. Mark is full of them, Q contains them, and the record of Peter's earliest sermon calls Jesus a healer (see Acts 2:22). Miracle stories were not added onto other stories that had been around for years; they were part of the tradition from the beginning. This suggests that something must have happened, no matter how we interpret them today.

However, some think there has been an element of exaggeration, or rewriting. Some scholars feel that some of the sayings of Jesus were probably not said by him, but were placed on his lips by the evangelists. (Perhaps they made them up; perhaps they thought the risen Jesus was speaking to them.) This is rather like journalists who report for newspapers. They will sometimes make up a quotation that they think sums up the feelings of a person.

Other Christians disagree, and feel that all the sayings are from Jesus.

Take the lengthy speeches about Jesus as the bread of life in John 6, for example. Some think these were composed by John to tell people what he thought about Jesus, and were based upon his deep beliefs. He might have been thinking about the meaning of the holy Communion, with the bread and the wine representing Jesus (see John 6:53–8). Then again, Jesus might have said all these things himself!

The Gospels Today

In Worship

The Gospels are read in Church services to remember the words of Jesus. Some Churches do this with great dramatic style. The book of the Gospels is carried in procession along the Church, accompanied by people holding candles, and also swinging perfumed incense. The candles and incense honour Christ who is God and the Light of the world. The book is lifted up to show how important the words of Jesus are.

A Catholic Gospel procession.

In Prayer

Christians read through the Gospels as they pray, thinking about the words, and asking God to speak through them. Some people take a saying of Jesus and repeat it over and over again to themselves, letting the truth of it sink in. Others imagine that they are in one of the stories, and they meditate, imagining that Jesus speaks to them as one of the characters.

In Discussion

A home Bible Study.

Some Christians meet in each other's homes to read through the Scriptures and talk about them. They will ask questions about things they do not understand, and seek to apply the words to their daily lives.

Activities

Key Elements

1 What language did Jesus speak?

2 Did disciples memorise their rabbi's teaching?

3 a) What is an eyewitness?
b) What have eyewitnesses got to do with the reliability of the Gospels?

4 Why is it significant that the words of Jesus appear as rimes in the Aramaic?

5 How early were miracle stories told about Jesus?

6 What is happening in the photograph at the top of p. 13?

7 How are the Gospels used in prayer and discussion?

Think About It

8 If the evangelists put some words onto the lips of Jesus, did they mean to lie?

9 What is your opinion of the accuracy of the Gospels?

Assignments

10 Some members of the class might like to try a Gospel meditation.

a) Choose a passage, e.g. Mark 2:1–11. Read it through. Do you identify with anyone in particular?

b) Relax and sit comfortably. Breath steadily, eyes closed for a few minutes.

c) Start to imagine the beginning of the scene in your mind. As it comes alive, all sorts of things might happen. The scene might change to somewhere familiar to you. You might find yourself as one of the people. Let it happen, like a waking dream.

d) When you think it is ended, sit quietly and breath steadily again, then open your eyes. Talk to others about what they felt.

11 Imagine that the people in the picture start going to a Church to find out about God. They join a Bible study group. About half the members are elderly. They read Matthew 22:34–40. What might they think of this? How might other members of the group feel about this?

The Power of the Gospels

Some people have been challenged and changed by what they have read in the Gospels. Here are some examples.

Bruce Kent, a former Roman Catholic priest, led peace marches for CND, the Campaign for Nuclear Disarmament, in the 1980s.

Happy are those who work for peace; God will call them his children. (Matthew 5:9)

Cliff Richard, singer and entertainer, made a commitment to Christ in the early 1960s after he had risen to fame.

'No one can enter the Kingdom of God unless he is born of water and the Spirit.' (John 3:5)

Corrie Ten Boom was sent to a concentration camp in the Second World War for sheltering Jewish refugees in Holland.

The greatest love a person can have for his friends is to give his life for them. (John 15:13)

Spotlight on Kris Akabusi

Kris Akabusi, international athlete, and Gold Medal Winner, is a committed Christian. As he was rising to fame, he was very materialistic, wanting many possessions. He wanted the best. He changed cars regularly, once owning a Mercedes, but only to be overtaken by someone in a better model, and so he yearned for a bigger and better car again!

In 1986, he was in his hotel room in Edinburgh for the Commonwealth Games. He picked up a copy of the *Good News Bible*, donated by the National Bible Society of Scotland to every room. He read and read, and was fascinated. In the Gospels he found a man who was brave, powerful, and willing to make sacrifices. He was strong, but not the 'macho' type who dare not show their feelings. He was amazed at the courage of the man who went back to Jerusalem,

Kris Akabusi in the 400m hurdles.

knowing that the authorities would crucify him.

He was challenged by what he read about Jesus. He thought about Christianity for ten months, asking questions, and reading books, until he felt convinced that Jesus was real. The final decision came when he thought about his birthday, 28 November 1958. The years were numbered after Jesus' birth, and that struck him. 'Jesus had to be the main man', he said.

He prayed, 'Lord, if you're there and I really don't know if you are, you'd better come and say "Hi" to Kris.' He was overwhelmed with a sense of God's presence, and has been involved in the 'Christians in Sport' movement ever since. He says that he has known a love and a security that he was searching for all his life.

Christians believe that Jesus is risen, and affects people today. It is important, therefore, in searching for evidence about him, to consider stories like that of Kris Akabusi. The words of Jesus challenged him, and he seeks to serve him as a result.

Questions

* How do you react to the above story? Talk about this as a class.
* What started Kris thinking about who Jesus was?

Vocabulary

Gospel   Aramaic
evangelion   rabbi
synoptic
Q
Rylands Fragment
Codex Sinaiticus
Gabbatha

2

Land of Promise

- Abraham's covenant
- Map of the land
- Features of the land and key places
- The Torah
- Circumcision
- Prayer

- The Temple
- Roman rule
- Groups: Sadducees, Pharisees, Essenes, Zealots
- Jews and Christians through the ages

LOOK UP AT THE STARS IN THE SKY... CAN YOU NUMBER THEM?

NO.

THUS SHALL THE NUMBER OF YOUR DESCENDENTS BE!

HOW WILL I KNOW THIS WILL BE?

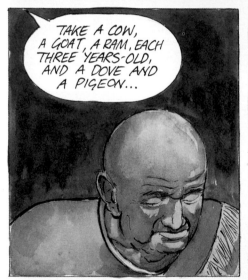

TAKE A COW, A GOAT, A RAM, EACH THREE YEARS-OLD, AND A DOVE AND A PIGEON...

THE ANIMALS WERE SACRIFICED AND CUT IN HALF. THEY WERE LINED UP IN TWO ROWS.

ABRAHAM FELL INTO A DEEP SLEEP, AND WAS TROUBLED BY DREAMS OF HOW HIS DESCENDENTS WOULD SUFFER IN THE FUTURE.

A BURNING TORCH AND SMOKING POT PASSES IN BETWEEN THE SACRIFICES. GOD WAS CONFIRMING HIS SPECIAL AGREEMENT.

The modern city of Jerusalem, and the land of Israel and its neighbours. A land of great beauty, full of ancient history, but also locked in conflict, as two ancient peoples contend for the land, Jews and Palestinians, most of whom are Muslims. The modern state of Israel was set up in 1948. Before this time, a few Jewish settlers lived in the land, among the Palestinians. Yet, many centuries earlier, much of the land had belonged to the Jews. They were scattered among the nations when the Romans defeated the Jews in a war that led to the destruction of Jerusalem and the setting up of a pagan temple there. The land was still theirs, in their eyes, for it was a land of promise, given to them by God.

Abraham's Promise

The Hebrew Bible, in the Book of Genesis, tells the story of the great ancestor of the Jews, Abraham. He was called by God to leave his homeland in the area of modern day Iraq/Iran and he journeyed to Canaan, as Palestine/Israel was then known.

Various promises are made to him:

'I will bless those who bless you,
But I will curse those who curse you.
And through you I will bless all the
nations.' (Genesis 12:3)

He is promised many descendants, as many as the stars in the sky. He makes a covenant (a special, solemn agreement) with God, sacrificing a cow, a goat, a ram, a dove and a pigeon, to seal this by blood (an ancient custom). Then the promise is given about the land:

'I promise to give your descendants all this land
from the border of Egypt to the River Euphrates...

(Read Genesis 12:1–9; 15)

Many years later, Israel had split into two kingdoms. The southern one, Judah, survived.

Many of the northern tribes were lost when the Assyrians deported them. Galilee was settled by Jews after many had returned from a time in Babylon, and re-developed Judaea. Samaria was non-Jewish, populated by the descendants of the foreigners brought there by the Assyrians when they deported the tribes of Israel. The Samaritans followed part of the Jewish religion, having their own holy mountain, Gerazim, and the Law of Moses.

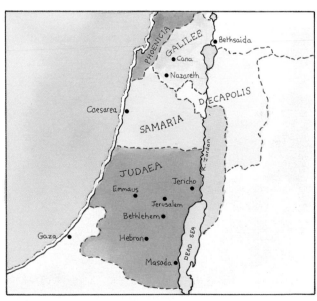

How the land was divided at the time of Jesus.

Certain places are important in the Gospels:

▶ **Jerusalem** – the holy city because the Jewish Temple stood there.

▶ **Bethlehem** – Two of the Gospels say that Jesus was born here.

▶ **Nazareth** – Jesus was brought up here, probably working as a carpenter or builder.

▶ **River Jordan** – Jesus was baptised here by the preacher John the Baptist.

▶ **Capernaum** – Jesus preached here, and stayed there during his ministry.

What Sort of Land?

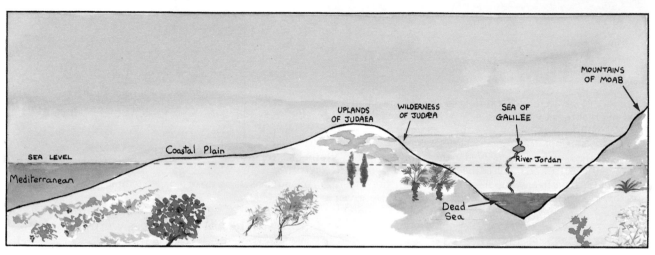

This cross-section of the land shows how varied the landscape is for such a small country. There are deserts, high mountains (sometimes with snow), lush valleys and fertile plains near the coast. The Sea of Galilee is completely enclosed, like a huge lake, and the larger Dead Sea is so-called because nothing lives in it. It is highly salty and has no outlet.

Snapshots

This land was described in the Hebrew Bible as 'flowing with milk and honey', in other words very fertile and habitable.

The wilderness in Israel.

Floating in the Dead Sea.

The Torah

Modern Jews carrying the Torah scrolls. The insert shows an actor playing the part of Moses.

The Jewish faith has always been based upon the *Torah*, the Law, given by Moses. Moses led the Hebrews (ancestors of the Jews) out of slavery in Egypt in about 1300BCE. This is known as the Exodus. The people assembled at a holy mountain, Sinai, where Moses went to pray and meditate. He came down with two stone tablets bearing the Ten Commandments, and other laws were added to these (making 613 in total). The laws, and stories of the the early Hebrews are contained in the five books of Moses; Genesis, Exodus, Leviticus, Numbers and Deuteronomy.

Torah also means 'way' in Hebrew. Devout Jews study the Torah to find how they should live their lives. In their synagogue services the scrolls of the Torah are carried in procession from the special chamber, the Ark, where they are kept.

Circumcision

Jewish male babies are circumcised at eight days after birth. This means that the foreskin of the penis is cut away. This is not only for health reasons, but as a sign of the covenant between God and the Jews. It is a very ancient custom, practised by Abraham and Moses.

The child is brought into the room and the people cry out 'Blessed is he! Blessed is he!' A *Mohel* (circumciser) performs the circumcision, and then the child is given a few drops of wine

to calm it. The child is lifted up, and these words are said:

> *Blessed are you, Lord our God, King of the universe, who has sanctified us with his commandments and commanded us to enter my son into the covenant with Abraham.*

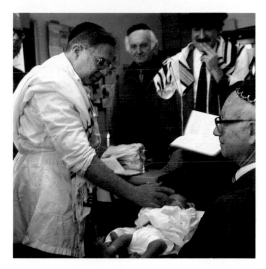

Jewish circumcision ceremony.

Prayer

This Jewish boy is praying. He has a small leather box strapped to his forehead and his left arm. These are called phylacteries or *tefillin*. The boxes contain portions of the Torah. One contains the *Shema*, the Jewish statement of faith; 'Hear O Israel, the Lord our God, the Lord is one.' The other contains some words from Exodus 13:1–16. The origin of this custom is the instruction that the words of the Torah should always be in the head and the heart, when people rise and when they sleep. (This originally meant 'Think about the Law all the time.')

Activities

Key Elements

1 Who was Abraham?

2 What does covenant mean?

3 What was promised to Abraham?

4 How did Abraham seal the covenant?

5 Who were the Samaritans?

6 What significance did Jerusalem, Bethlehem, Nazareth, the River Jordan, and Capernaum have for Jesus?

7 What does Torah mean?

8 Who was Moses?

9 What happened at Mount Sinai?

10 How many laws are there in the Torah?

11 What is circumcision?

12 Why do Jews practise circumcision?

13 Why do Jewish men wear phylacteries when they pray?

14 a) Write out the Shema.
    b) Why is the Shema important?

Assignment

15 Design a travel brochure, describing the different sorts of climate and landscape in modern day Israel.

The Temple

A model of the Temple in Jerusalem.

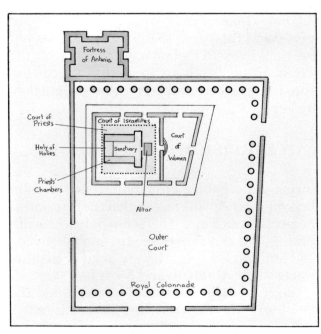

The Temple at the time of Jesus.

The Temple in Jesus' time was a huge, imposing building in Jerusalem. This had been extended by King Herod with fortifications and outer courts. Originally, there was a court for the Israelites, and the Holy Place, which only the priests could enter. There had been an earlier Temple, built by King Solomon, but the Babylonians had destroyed this. Moses started the first Temple, or Tabernacle, in a tent with poles around it.

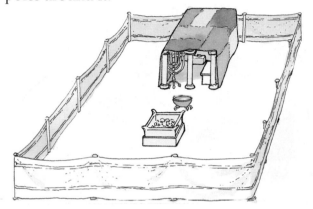

The first Temple or Tabernacle.

The altar of sacrifice stood before the Holy Place, and in the outer part of the tent, there was a lampstand, an incense altar and a table for a bread offering. In the Holy of Holies, which only the High Priest could enter at certain times, was the Ark of the Covenant, an ornate box that originally contained the tablets of the Torah. The Jews believed that the presence of God, the *Shekinah*, hovered over this in a special way.

The Ark of the Covenant, as it was shown in the film *Raiders of the Lost Ark*.

Raiders of the Lost Ark used the fact that no one knows what happened to the Ark, as a story for the film. When the Romans conquered Judaea, they did not find it in the Holy of Holies. Perhaps it was lost in ancient Babylon.

The Court of the Gentiles was the outer court, and a non-Jew could go no further on pain of death. The Romans allowed the death sentence to be passed by the Jewish leaders on anyone trespassing in this way. A warning sign has been found in the ruins of the Temple. This says:

No stranger may enter within the balustrade or embankment round the Temple. Anyone caught doing so will bear the responsibility for his own ensuing death.

70CE

Jerusalem was beseiged and fell in 70CE. The Temple was destroyed by the Romans after the war with the Jews. The Romans destroyed the Temple because they knew how important this was for the Jews, and they carried off its treasures. The sculpture below shows them carrying away the *menorah*, the large lampstand in the Holy Place.

All that remains of this once great building is the Western Wall, also known as the Wailing Wall (see p.109). Many Jews go here on pilgrimage to pray, sometimes leaving written prayers lodged into the cracks in the stones.

Romans carrying off Temple treasures.

Activities

Key Elements

1 Draw a diagram of the layout of the Temple and label it.

2 List all the things kept in the Holy Place.

3 What was kept in the Ark?

4 Why do you think there was a Holy Place in the Temple?

5 What might happen if a non-Jew went into the inner courts?

6 Why did the Romans destroy the Temple in 70CE?

7 Which part of it is still standing?

Think About It

8 Why do you think modern Jews travel to the Western Wall?

Politics

The Roman general, Pompey, marched his troops into Jerusalem in 63BCE, entering the Holy Place in the Temple, in defiance. From that time, the Jews had been under Roman rule. At first, the Romans allowed a measure of independence. They allowed kings to rule over Judaea, giving the title first of all to Herod the Great (40–4BCE). He was not a popular ruler, as he was cruel and tried to please the Romans. He re-built the Temple, but he also built Roman temples, and a harbour town named after the Emperor, Caesarea, which had a huge amphitheatre. He had members of his own family executed.

The rule of kings ended in 6CE because of Judas the Galilean. This man led a revolt against the Romans. Josephus writes this:

Judas prevailed with his countrymen to revolt; and said they were cowards if they would endure to pay a tax to the Romans, and would, after God, submit to mortal men as their lords. (Jewish Wars)

The amphitheatre at Caesarea.

Judaea was then under a procurator (governor), and Pontius Pilate was the procurator responsible for the arrest and execution of Jesus.

Galilee remained under the Herodians, though. Herod Antipas was ruler over Galilee during the ministry of Jesus. He was one of four *tetrachs* who ruled over the area.

Roman rule was not popular, though new buildings, roads and educational opportunities were introduced. Many believed that the land was theirs, given by God. Jews were exempt from sacrificing to the Emperor to prove their loyalty, but they hated paying taxes to Caesar,

A coin showing the head of Caesar.

and they could be called upon to assist soldiers in various ways. A person could be stopped and asked to carry a burden for as much as a Roman mile, for example.

Groups

Judaism was divided between different religious and political groups at the time of Jesus.

The Pharisees

This was the largest group, numbering about 6,000 in the first century CE. They probably derived from a group who opposed Greek rulers and refused to compromise the Torah by not eating pork and by not working on the Sabbath. Their name might come from a Hebrew word 'to separate'. They accepted all the books of the Hebrew Bible as Scripture, but also used an oral tradition of commentary on the Torah, with its own laws, as important. They believed in the resurrection of the body and angels. They were respected by the ordinary people, and Jesus had influential friends amongst them. He criticised their emphasis on the oral Law, and attacked some of their concern with external purity when purity of the heart was what mattered.

The Sadducees

They were a much smaller, but powerful group. They were the landed gentry, the wealthy, and had a great deal of influence in politics, occupying many seats on the Sanhedrin, the Greater Council of the Jews. (This had 70 members and was presided over by the High Priest.) They accepted only the Torah as Scripture, and did not believe in resurrection. They were concerned to keep the status quo and maintain peace with Rome.

Zealots

This group was filled with zeal for the Torah, and believed that no foreign power should rule the land that God had given them. They were prepared to use terrorist actions and fight a war to drive the Romans out. They might not have formed a distinct party but members of the

Pharisees and Essenes could also be Zealots if they held these strict political ideas.

Essenes

Josephus refers to this group as the third philosophy of the Jews. They lived a monastic life, along with lay members who lived near the monasteries. They wrote commentaries on the Scriptures and withdrew from the Temple, believing its administration to be corrupt. They expected an imminent crisis, and a war to drive the Romans out of the land. One of their communities was probably at Qumran, near the Dead Sea. The Dead Sea Scrolls were found in caves, stored in clay jars in this area. They are ancient scrolls containing commentaries and portions of Scripture.

The Scribes are also mentioned in the Gospels. They were lawyers or rabbis who were trained in the Torah, and copied this out. Many would have belonged to the Pharisees.

The atmosphere at the time of Jesus was electric. Many people were expecting a great leader to arise who would help them fight the Romans and win back their land. Some thought that God would intervene, and wonderful, supernatural things were going to happen.

The ruins at Qumran.

Activities

Key Elements

1 When did the Jews come under Roman rule?

2 Why did Pompey enter the Holy Place?

3 Who was the first King of the Jews approved by the Romans?

4 Why did the Romans introduce procurators into Judaea after 6CE?

5 List the four groups found amongst the Jews at the time of Jesus.

6 Write a paragraph about each group saying how they differed from one another.

Think About It

7 Imagine that you are a Zealot. Try to argue with people who are about to pay their tax to Caesar.

8 Why do you think some people joined the Essenes?

Assignment

9   Find a sentence for each of the people below that sums up their points of view.

Jews and Christians through the Ages

The first Christians were all Jews; Jesus was a Jew, the 12 apostles were, and if Peter was the first Pope, as is traditionally believed by the Catholic Church, then the first Pope was Jewish! Jesus would have had no intention of starting a new faith. He wanted to revive and change an old one. For him, the Jews were the chosen race, who had received the Torah and the promises of the coming Kingdom. Though the Kingdom was open to anyone, it was to be offered to the Jews first. This is essentially the same viewpoint that we see in the rest of the New Testament. Yet, before too long, the two faiths separated. More and more Gentiles were becoming Christians, and they were not expected to keep all the laws that Jewish believers were used to keeping. After 70CE, and the fall of Jerusalem, the rabbis were suspicious of the Christians. They could attend synagogue in most places, but they had no influence or authority in Jewish life and worship.

Gradually, when Rome embraced Christianity as its official faith in the fourth century CE, many Christians began to call the Jews 'Christ killers' and accuse them of 'deicide' (killing God). This led to mockery and persecution. Many Jews were expelled from countries, and could only work in certain areas. During the Middle Ages, some countries forced Jews to wear the yellow star of David. This persecution was totally misguided, as technically, it was mainly the Romans who had killed Jesus, along with only some of the Jewish leaders.

A tale was told in the Middle Ages of a Jewish cobbler called Ahasver. He is said to have cursed Christ on the way to the cross. He was condemned to wander restlessly, from age to age, until Christ's return. It is not mentioned in the Bible, at all. It summed up the hatred and suspicion that many felt towards the Jews at the time. The Jewish people were wanderers without a homeland of their own, though they tried their best to settle in a country and work hard as good citizens.

The ultimate persecution came in Hitler's Germany when 6 million Jews were killed in concentration camps. The Nazis spoke of a 'Final Solution' that would rid the world of Jews! Many people alive today lost members of their family in the camps.

One sad story sums up the prejudice and fear that many people used to have. Some Jews had been shot and dumped in a pit in Germany. They were left for dead. One young man was alive, and crawled out at night. He made his way to a farmhouse. The farmer's wife asked if he was a Jew, because they deserved what came to them. He thought quickly and replied, 'No, I am your Saviour Jesus Christ come down from the cross. I have come to see if you will welcome me.' He got the help he needed.

Jewish prisoners at Buchenwald concentration camp during the Second World War 1939–45.

Christians have tried to make up for their wrong attitudes in the past. The Roman Catholic Church has declared its mistake in persecuting Jews in the past, and has issued a statement respecting Judaism as a living religion which has much in common with its own. Groups of Jews and Christians meet to discuss and pray.

There were individuals who stood out from the crowd in the past, too, such as Wichard von Bredow, District President of the district of Schlossberg, in Germany.

On the 10 November 1938, von Bredow received a teletype informing him that all the synagogues in Germany were being burned. The police and the fire brigade were not to intervene. He put on his army uniform and said farewell to his wife. 'I am going to the synagogue in Schierwindt, and as a Christian and a German mean to prevent one of the greatest crimes within my jurisdiction. I cannot do otherwise.'

He knew he risked being sent to a concentration camp.

He stood in front of the synagogue and drew his pistol on the people who were trying to burn it. They withdrew. This synagogue was the only one in the area to remain standing. No one dared resist the District President.

Corrie Ten Boom and her family hid Jewish refugees in occupied Holland, until being sent to the camps by the Gestapo. Many others died or suffered in the same way, and their names are remembered in a memorial in Jerusalem at Yad Vashem, which is a museum keeping alive the terrible memory of the holocaust.

A memorial to murdered Jews at Yad Vashem.

Some modern Jews have actually started to follow Jesus as Messiah (i.e. the coming King) but they do not call themselves Christians. They call themselves Messianic Jews. They use the New Testament, believe everything about Jesus that Christians do, but are careful to keep their Jewish heritage and customs. They are cautious about using the word 'Christian'; it is too dirty a word in Jewish folk-memory. After all, many of the guards at the camps called themselves' Christians'.

The Jewish community is very unsure what to make of these Jews. Are they betraying their faith or trying to enrich it?

The singer Helen Shapiro is a Messianic Jew. One of her songs from a recent album, *Kadosh*, is to 'Messiah King! Yeshua Lord! My salvation!'

Messianic Jews call Jesus *Yeshua*. This is the Hebrew version of his name, and it is often written as follows:

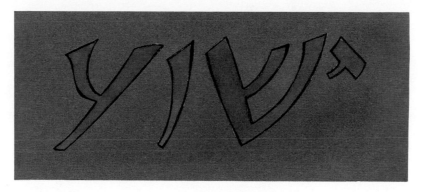

Activities

Key Elements

1 What religion was Jesus?

2 What does *'deicide'* mean?

3 What was the yellow star?

4 What was the 'Final Solution'?

5 What is Yad Vashem?

6 What is a Messianic Jew?

Think About It

7 Why do you think the Jews were persecuted in the past? What might have been done to stop this?

8 Why do you think the story of the wandering Jew was so popular in the Middle Ages?

9 Why do you think Messianic Jews do not readily call themselves Christians?

Assignment

10 Write a radio play based upon the story of Wichard von Bredow. Record this on tape.

Vocabulary

covenant	phylactery	Sadducee
Torah	Western Wall	Pharisee
circumcision	Holy Place	Essene
tefillin	Zealot	Messianic Jew

3

Lifeline One
Birth to Baptism

- Jesus' date of birth
- The Christmas story as seen in cards, cribs and carols
- The birth stories in Matthew and Luke
- Prophecies
- History versus myth
- The Magnificat
- The presentation of Jesus and the Nunc Dimittis

- Christmas worship today
- The boyhood of Jesus and questioning the Scribes
- *Bar Mitzvah*
- John the Baptist
- The Baptism of Jesus
- Christian baptism today

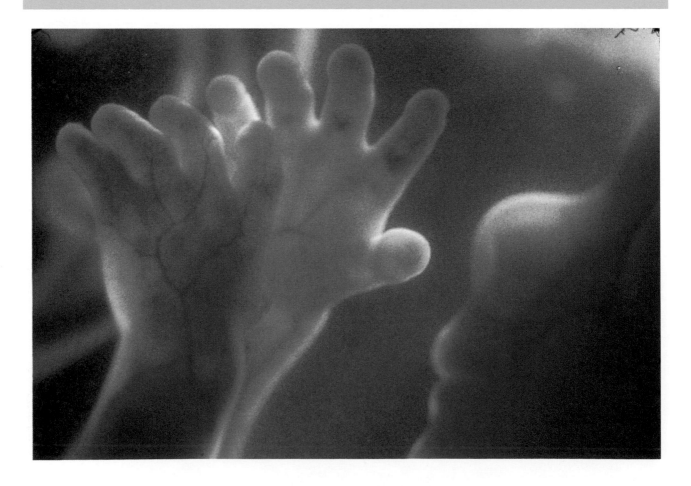

THE TIME IS NEAR, YOSIF! I CAN FEEL THE PAINS

HOLD ON MIRIAM... NOT MUCH FURTHER NOW...

SOMETIME IN THE REIGN OF THE EMPEROR AUGUSTUS, A FAMILY MAKES ITS WAY TO BETHLEHEM IN JUDAEA.

'AN IMPERIAL CENSUS, EVERYONE TO RETURN TO THE TOWN OF BIRTH... OF ALL THE TIMES IT HAD TO COME!'

DO NOT BE AFRAID TO TAKE MIRIAM AS YOUR WIFE, YOSIF! NO MAN HAS TOUCHED HER...

'I WAS ABOUT TO SEND HER AWAY WHEN I FOUND OUT SHE WAS PREGNANT... BUT THEN THE VISIONS IN THE NIGHT CAME...'

AND I BELIEVED THE VOICE OF GOD'S ANGEL...

'I REMEMBER HOW IT ALL BEGAN, BEFORE THE CHILD FIRST MOVED, BEFORE THE PAIN...'

WHO ARE YOU?

YOU ARE HIGHLY FAVOURED MIRIAM... THE SPIRIT WILL COME UPON YOU AND OVERSHADOW YOU SO THAT THE CHILD BORN WILL BE HOLY...

AND SO THIS IS HOW THE NEW KING IS TO BE BORN INTO THE WORLD, IN THIS MESS?

Note

Miriam and Yosif are the Hebrew forms of Mary and Joseph.

The Birth of Jesus

No one knows for certain Jesus' date of birth. Matthew says that Herod was king of the Jews. He died in 4BCE. We know that the Christian dating scheme is wrong, because a monk made a mistake. Jesus was therefore born BCE! How soon before 4BCE is uncertain. It might have been as early as 8BCE. In that case, if he died in 30 or 33CE, as is probable, then he would have been around 38 or 41 years old when he died.

The figures in the colourful crib above are taken from the Gospel stories. Mary, mother of Jesus, the baby, Joseph his father, visiting shepherds, worshipping wise men (often shown as kings). It is a quaint, familiar scene, almost sentimental. Childhood carols like 'Away in a manger' reinforce this:

> Away in a manger, no crib for a bed,
> The little Lord Jesus laid down his sweet head.
> The stars in the bright sky looked down where
> he lay,
> The little Lord Jesus asleep on the hay.

The original story tries to tell something dramatic, shocking and awesome! Take these two verses from other well-known carols:

> Christ, by highest heaven adored,
> Christ, the everlasting Lord,
> Late in time behold him come,
> Offspring of a virgin's womb!
> Veiled in flesh the Godhead see,
> Hail the incarnate Deity!
> Pleased as man with man to dwell,
> Jesus, our Emmanuel!

> God of God,
> Light of light,
> Lo! he abhors not the Virgin's womb;
> Very God,
> Begotten not created:
> O come, let us adore him,
> Christ the Lord.

The story tells about God, creator of the universe, stepping into his own creation, the timeless one coming in time. It is like an author writing himself into one of his novels. Christians believe that God became a human being in Jesus (they use the special word 'incarnation' for this, meaning 'in a body'). He came in a powerful way, born of a virgin who had had no sexual relations with any man.

The Gospel Accounts

The story of the birth of Jesus is related in only two of the Gospels; Matthew and Luke. Mark is silent about his early years, starting the story from the start of his public ministry. John talks about God becoming human in Jesus, but gives no details. In the rest of the New Testament, Paul mentions his birth only once, stating that, 'he came as the son of a human mother', Galatians 4:4, that is all.

Matthew and Luke tell different stories, although they agree on the central details.

Matthew

(Chapter 1:18–2:23)

*Joseph is engaged to Mary, and finds that she is pregnant. He is about to dismiss her when an angel visits him in a dream and tells him that she is a virgin. He is to call the child Jesus.

*Wise men come from the east, following the star. They visit King Herod and ask advice. They learn that the Scriptures say that Messiah will be born in Bethlehem.

*The angel warns Joseph to escape to Egypt. Meanwhile, Herod has all the children, two years old and younger, killed.

*Joseph and family return from Egypt when Herod dies. He is afraid to return to Judaea, and they settle in Nazareth.

Luke

(Chapter 1:26–38; 2:1–20)

*The angel Gabriel appears to Mary to tell her that she has been specially chosen and she will give birth to Jesus, even though she is a virgin. This greeting is known as the Annunciation, from the Latin word that gives us 'announce'.

*Joseph and family travel to Bethlehem because of a census ordered by Emperor Augustus. Mary gave birth in a stable.

*The shepherds hear the message of the angels and come to worship the new born child.

The well-known stories of the wise men and the shepherds come from two different Gospels. However, Matthew and Luke agree that Jesus was born of a virgin, in Bethlehem.

Comments upon the Birth Stories

• Joseph was betrothed to Mary. That was not quite being married, but stronger than engagement. Marriage contracts had been signed, but the couple were not fully married until the wedding night, when the marriage was consummated by sexual intercourse. To send her away, he would have had to divorce her, and he could have disgraced her publicly, and even had her stoned to death!

• Mary is described as a *parthenos* in the Greek of the New Testament. This could mean 'young girl' or 'virgin' depending upon the circumstances. From Luke 1:26–38, it clearly means 'virgin'. In v34 she protests that she is *parthenos*, so how could the angel's message be true?

• Many people believed in angels in New Testament times, and they were seen as messengers of God. It was common to believe they spoke in dreams. Gabriel was one of the Archangels, along with Michael and Raphael. 'Gabriel' means 'God is great'.

• Egypt was often used as a place of refuge by the Jews throughout their history – remember the story of Joseph and the Hebrews going there in a famine.

• Matthew's title for Jesus is *Immanuel*, from Isaiah 7:14; Luke calls Jesus 'Son of the Most High', meaning 'Son of God'; 'Saviour', 'Christ' (i.e. Messiah); and 'Lord', a title that could mean king or God.

The Hebrew Scriptures

Matthew is concerned to prove that the Hebrew Scriptures have been fulfilled in the events of Jesus' birth, often using the phrase, 'This was done to make what the Lord said through the prophet come true.'

There are a number of Scriptures that relate to the birth story of Matthew, such as;

▶ **Isaiah 7:14** – 'Well then, the Lord himself will give you a sign: a young woman who is pregnant will have a son and will name him "Immanuel".'

('Immanuel' means 'God is with us' in Hebrew.)

▶ **Micah 5:2** – 'The Lord says, "Bethlehem Ephrathah, you are one of the smallest towns in Judah, but out of you I will bring a ruler for Israel, whose family line goes back to ancient times".'

▶ **Numbers 24:17** – 'I look into the future, and I see the nation of Israel. A king, like a bright star, will arise in that nation. Like a comet he will come from Israel.'

▶ **Jeremiah 31:15** – 'A sound is heard in Ramah, the sound of bitter weeping...' was not meant to be a prophecy about the birth of the Messiah, but a comment upon the sufferings of the Jews at Jeremiah's time. Matthew has compared it to Herod's massacre, though.

▶ **Matthew 2:23** – 'He will be called a Nazarene' is not an actual Scripture. It is possible that Matthew is playing with words, here. In Hebrew, 'NZR' means 'branch', and there was a prophecy; 'Then a shoot shall grow from the stock of Jesse, and a branch shall spring from his roots. The Spirit of the Lord shall rest upon him...'

Many Christians understand the stories in Matthew and Luke as history, as fact. That is how Jesus was born; it is different and special because it was a unique event. God became man.

Some question some of the stories. They see the stories as later interpretations of who Jesus was, rather than a report of historical events. They use symbols, and myths, to draw out the mystery and majesty of Jesus. Such Christians believe that Jesus was God; but they think he was born in a normal way. The stories were made up, like stories with a moral. This man, they are saying, is really God!

History Versus Myth

The Virgin Birth

• **Person 1**: This story sounds like the old Greek myths! Alexander the Great was said to have been born because a god had sex with his mother! We can't believe this today. Ancient people told stories like this about really special people. The early Christians were just trying to say how great Jesus was. The prophecy in Isaiah 7:14 uses the Hebrew word for 'young woman', which does not necessarily mean 'virgin'.

- **Person 2**: I disagree. The birth of Jesus is very different from other birth stories told by Greeks or Romans. God did not have sex with Mary; he performed a miracle in her womb to conceive Jesus. He gave her a choice, too; the old myths had gods tricking women all the time! As for Isaiah, the Hebrew for 'young woman' can mean 'virgin' sometimes.
- **Person 1**: But a virgin birth is a scientific impossibility. Even if it happened, then the child would be female, because a woman only carries certain genes.
- **Person 2**: That all depends on whether you believe in the supernatural and miracles, doesn't it! With God, anything is possible...

The Star and the Wise Men

- **Person 3**: I think the star is just a symbol. Ancient people told stories about special stars appearing at the birth of emperors and special people. The early Christians told such a story about Jesus. It meant he was really special. Matthew probably got the idea from the old prophecy about a comet or star rising out of Israel.
- **Person 4**: Hang on, ancient records from China and Babylon show that there was some unusual activity around 7–4BCE. There were comets, and a conjunction of Jupiter and Saturn, where they were in line in the sky, they would have appeared as a bright star.
- **Person 3**: Maybe, but that doesn't prove that they were **the** star... And the wise men brought symbolic gifts, gold for a king, frankincense for a god, and myrrh for a burial. The gifts were made up by Matthew to make the point that Jesus was King, God, and was destined to die on a cross.
- **Person 4**: So they are symbolic... but why couldn't the wise men have intended them to be? The Greek word for 'wise men' is *magi* meaning 'stargazer'. This suggests they were real people travelling from the east, having seen a comet or new star.

The Census

- **Person 1**: Would people have had to travel to their homeland if there was a census? The only definite evidence that we have from Roman history about a census in Augustus' reign was in 6CE. This would have been too late for the birth of Jesus. Luke says that Quirinius was governor of Syria, which was in 6CE but not any earlier!
- **Person 2**: There is some evidence that people had to move back to their town of birth. We know from Egyptian records that a census was held there every 14 years. If this held true for Syria and Palestine too, then there would have been one in 8BCE, which would have been around the time of the birth of Jesus. Archaeology has revealed that Quirinius was in Syria between 10–7 BCE, but he does not seem to have been governor. Some say Luke can be read as meaning 'before Quirinius was governor', in the Greek, showing that he meant an earlier census.

Interview

IT IS A BEAUTIFUL BUT MADE-UP STORY, TRYING TO TELL US HOW JESUS IS SPECIAL. I DO BELIEVE HE WAS GOD LIVING AS ONE OF US, BUT THE STORIES ARE JUST FIRST-CENTURY WAYS OF EXPRESSING THIS.

I TOO BELIEVE THAT JESUS WAS GOD MADE MAN, BUT I DO NOT FEEL THAT I NEED TO QUESTION THE STORIES AS MUCH AS MY LEARNED FRIEND HERE. I THINK GOD CAME INTO THIS WORLD IN A SPECIAL WAY; THE VIRGIN BIRTH WAS A SIGN THAT SOMETHING NEW AND REMARKABLE WAS HAPPENING.

Other Stories Surrounding the Birth

Luke contains two extra stories about the family of Jesus at the time of his birth. The first concerns Mary before she gave birth, and the second is when Jesus was taken to the Temple as an eight-day-old child.

Mary's Song
(Luke 1:39–56)

Mary went to stay with her cousin, Elizabeth, after seeing the vision of the angel. Elizabeth was also pregnant with the future John the Baptist. Elizabeth felt the child move in her womb when Mary entered, and she felt that something special had happened to her cousin. She said, 'You are the most blessed of all women, and blessed is the child you will bear! Why should this great thing happen to me, that my Lord's mother comes to visit me?' Mary responded by singing a hymn of praise, called the 'Magnificat', from the Latin words for the opening of the hymn:

> *My heart praises the Lord;*
> *my soul is glad because of God my Saviour,*
> *for he has remembered me, his lowly servant!*
> *From now on all people will call me happy,*
> *because of the great things the*
> *Mighty God has done for me.*
> *His name is holy;*
> *from one generation to another*
> *he shows mercy to those who honour him.*
> *He has stretched out his mighty arm*
> *and scatters the proud with all their plans.*
> *He has brought down mighty kings from their thrones,*
> *and lifted up the lowly.*
> *He has filled the hungry with good things,*
> *and sent the rich away with empty hands.*
> *He has kept the promise he made to our ancestors,*
> *and has come to the help of his servant Israel.*
> *He has remembered to show mercy to Abraham*
> *and to his descendants for ever! (Luke 1:46–56)*

This praises God for remembering the fortunes of his people Israel, and for being on the side of the poor and down trodden, rather than the rich, as seen in the choice of a simple girl from Nazareth.

Some think this hymn might have originated in early Christian Churches in Judaea, and was put onto the lips of Mary by Luke. This is only a theory and many assume it is Mary's song. It is still sung in Christian worship today.

The Magnificat is usually sung in Anglican Evensong, a set form of Evening Prayer.

The Magnificat declares that God wants justice in his world. Some Christians use the ideas in this song to justify their involvement in politics and protest movements.

Christians holding a service on Easter Sunday, during the London to Aldermaston CND Easter March.

The Presentation of Jesus in the Temple
(Luke 2:22–38)

The Jewish custom was to take children to the Temple in Jerusalem on their eighth day, to present them to God in thanksgiving. Boys would be circumcised. Simeon took the child Jesus and was moved. He confessed him as the Messiah, and sang a song of thanksgiving, known as the 'Nunc Dimittis', again from the Latin words that open the song.

> Now, Lord, you have kept your promise,
> and you may let your servant go in peace.
> With my own eyes I have seen your salvation,
> which you have prepared in the presence of all peoples;
> A light to reveal your will to the Gentiles
> and bring glory to your people Israel.
> (Luke 2:29–32)

Simeon's song has been thought, by some, to be an early Jewish Christian hymn too, praising Jesus as the Messiah. This might be so, but many assume it is Simeon's song and see no reason to doubt this. There is a universalist belief in the song, that salvation will come from Jesus to Jews and non-Jews. Some Jews at the time believed that God's kingdom would only come for them.

The Nunc Dimittis is still sung in Christian worship.

Christmas Worship Today

Customs

Many of the customs associated with Christmas are pre-Christian in origin. The Christmas tree is of Viking origin. Evergreen trees were seen as magical because they kept their leaves in winter. The same was true of holly berries and mistletoe. Trees now have stars on top and holly berries are used in a carol as a symbol of Christ, in 'The Holly and the Ivy':

> The holly bears a berry,
> as red as any blood,
> and Mary bore sweet Jesus Christ
> to do poor sinners good.

Christmas trees were seen as symbols of the tree of Life, from the Garden of Eden story, when they were first used in Germany.

The Crib

The idea of making models of the figures in the birth stories, including the child in the manger, came from St Francis of Assisi (1181–1226). He was a friar, a travelling preacher, with a group of 'brothers'. He made a crib to teach the peasants of Italy (who could not read or write) about the birth of Jesus.

Some churches still have cribs at Christmas time. There might be a 'crib service' with songs and readings for young children, and they might perform a nativity play.

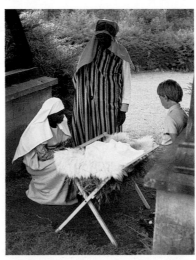

A scene from a nativity play.

Midnight Communion Services

Many Churches hold a midnight Communion service on Christmas Eve to start the day when the birth of Jesus is celebrated. Some of these are very formal, with white robes, candles and sweet-smelling incense. Some are very informal and friendly. Carols are sung throughout the service. The songs, the colours, and the joyfulness remember Jesus' birth, but sharing communion also remembers that he came to die.

Note

No one knows the actual date for the birth of Jesus. It was not 25 December. That was made his official birthday by the Roman Emperor Constantine, replacing an old Roman festival of the sun god, Saturnalia. If the story of the shepherds is true, then he would have been born around March, for the lambing season, when they would have to watch the flocks at night, is in spring time.

Activities

Key Elements

1 Who was the Roman Emperor when Jesus was born?

2 Read Matthew 1:18–2:23 and Luke 1:26–38; 2:1–20.
a) Where do Luke and Matthew agree and disagree in their telling of the birth of Jesus?
b) What message did the angel give to Joseph?
c) What is the 'Annunciation'?
d) What message did the angel give to Mary? What was her response?

3 a) What gifts did the wise men present to Jesus?
b) What did the gifts of the magi symbolise?

4 Where did Joseph and his family escape from Herod? What was Herod doing?

5 What ideas about Jesus are present (a) in Matthew and (b) in Luke? Comment on any titles given to Jesus.

6 What are the Magnficat and the Nunc Dimittis?

7 What problems are there in dating the census?

8 Read Exodus 1:15–2:10. How are the stories of the birth of Moses similar to those of the birth of Jesus?

Think About It

9 Discuss in groups the meaning behind the birth stories of Jesus.

10 Write a few paragraphs arguing for and against the virgin birth being a historical fact.

11 Look at the cartoon of the clergymen on p.35. Imagine that you are the interviewer. What further questions would you ask?

12 What do you think are the problems in trying to date the birth of Jesus?

13 Write either a nativity play designed to be performed by young children, or for teenagers, possibly for a school assembly.

14 Make a chart showing what customs and celebrations Christians use at Christmas. Use these headings:

Customs; Activities; Services.

The Boyhood of Jesus

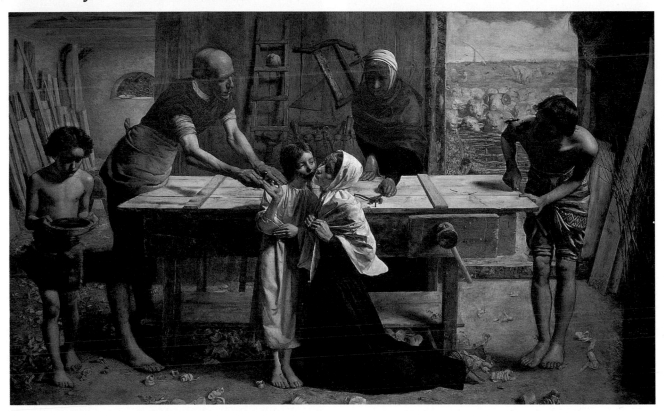

Christ in the House of his Parents, by Sir John Everett Millais.

The Gospels contain very little information about the childhood of Jesus. They are concerned mainly with his public ministry. Luke contains a story about Jesus aged 12 (Luke 2:41–52).

Jesus and his family had been on pilgrimage to Jerusalem for the Passover. Jesus stayed behind when his parents left, and they only realised he was missing after a day. On the third day, they found him in the Temple, talking to teachers of the Law who were amazed at his wisdom for one so young.

Jews were obliged to go to the Temple three times on pilgrimage, in the Hebrew Scriptures, at Passover, Pentecost and Tabernacles. At the time of Jesus, Jews living some distance away from Jerusalem were only expected to travel there at Passover.

Various details of the story surprise modern readers. Jesus seems to have been disobedient and disrespectful to his parents, and they seem to have been careless in leaving him behind.

Jesus, at 12, would have been at the end of his childhood in Jewish eyes. Today, at 13, Jewish boys undergo the *Bar Mitzvah* ceremony when they are considered as an adult in the affairs of religion. It is not clear how old this ceremony is (it is not in the Scriptures or other early Jewish writings like the *Talmud*). Jesus, though, was exerting his independence, and near adulthood in spiritual matters, by talking in the Temple. There is also a sense of the beginning of a detachment from his parents, stressing that God is his Father, 'Didn't you know that I had to be in my Father's house?' (Luke 2:49)

Mary and Jesus from Jacob Jordaens' *The Holy Family with St.John*.

This photograph shows a Jewish boy undergoing his Bar Mitzvah (meaning 'son of the commandments'). He has to study the Scriptures in Hebrew and read from them in the synagogue. After prayers, there is a party. He reads from the scrolls of the Law, the Torah, and is then able to form part of the *minyan* – the minimum of ten adults to form a synagogue congregation. Girls were unable to go through this ceremony until recently, when Reform Jews introduced the *Bat Mitzvah*, 'daughter of the commandments'.

Jesus' parents would not have noticed that he was missing for a day because it was the custom to travel with various members of the family, and they would have assumed that he was with other relatives in the caravan of baggage and animals.

Luke shows a sensitive interest in Mary, unlike the other evangelists. He has her singing the Magnificat, and stresses how she wonders at some of the things her child does. Luke 2:51 says, 'His mother treasured all these things in her heart.'

All Christians honour Mary as the mother of Jesus. Some also sing hymns in her honour, or ask for her prayers. This is frowned upon by other believers, for she is not God, they say. One title for her is *Theotokos* meaning 'God bearer' in Greek. She is honoured with this title because Christians believe she carried God in her womb.

Questions

* How old was Jesus when he stayed behind in the Temple?
* What did he say when his mother asked where he had been?
* What is a Bar Mitzvah?
* What is a minyan?
* How can Jesus' actions be defended against the charge that he was disobedient?
* Why were Mary and Joseph not negligent in leaving him behind?
* Imagine that you were one of the Teachers of the Law talking with Jesus in the Temple. Write a letter to another rabbi describing what happened and how you felt.

The Baptism of Jesus

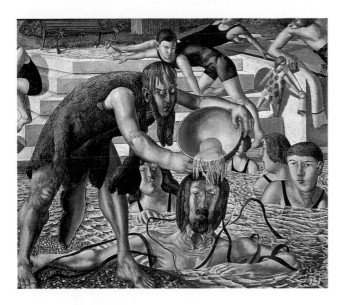

The baptism of Jesus painted by Stanley Spencer.

The turning point for Jesus was his baptism in the River Jordan. This would have been sometime in his late twenties or early thirties. Jesus was baptised by John the Baptist. The Gospels describe him as an ascetic prophet, dressing in camel-hair skins and a leather belt. He ate locusts and wild honey. He appears suddenly in Matthew and Mark, something of an enigma, a strange holy man. Luke has more background, describing his parents and his birth. According to Luke, John was the cousin of Jesus, born to Elizabeth and Zechariah (see Luke 1:5–25; 57–80). John is also mentioned by Josephus, the Jewish historian, as a preacher who called the people to repentance to prepare for God's Kingdom. That is how he is pictured in the Gospels. He compared himself to a person described in Isaiah, 'A voice cries out, "Prepare in the wilderness a road for the Lord! Clear the way in the desert for our God!"…'(Isaiah 40:3–5). John spoke of a coming deliverer, who would baptise 'with the Holy Spirit and fire'. He claimed that he was not worthy 'even to untie his sandals'.

We do not know exactly **how** John baptised; either it was by total immersion, plunging the person right under the water, or by pouring water over their heads as they stood or knelt in the water. John was making a striking point by urging Jews to be baptised. Converts to the Jewish faith had to undergo a baptism at the time, and his actions could have been seen as insulting by some. He was saying the people were 'unclean' before God, full of sin. He was calling them to turn back, and go through a symbolic washing. In fact, there were various types of 'baptist' groups around at the time, such as the Qumran community near the Dead Sea. They practised frequent bathing to purify themselves.

John the Baptist's dress is probably mentioned by the evangelists to compare him with Elijah, whom Jewish tradition said would come before the Messiah to warn people.

Jesus came to be baptised by John. Only Matthew seems to find this surprising as Jesus was the sinless Son of God to Christian believers. He has John saying: 'I ought to be baptised by you, and yet you have come to me!' Jesus replies, 'Let it be so for now. For in this way we shall do all that God requires.' (Matthew 3:14–15) Jesus probably accepted John's baptism to stand in solidarity with him, and his call to repentance. This was to be a feature of Jesus' own preaching ('Turn away from your sins and believe the Good News!' Mark 1:15)

Jesus had an intense religious experience at this time. He heard a voice, confirming him as the Son, or Messiah, and the Spirit came upon him, and this appeared symbolically as a dove. The Synoptic Gospels state that it was Jesus who saw the vision of the dove; John suggests that John the Baptist saw it, too. Jesus withdrew to the desert wilderness for a period of time (about 40 days) and then appeared preaching the Kingdom of God.

Christian Baptism Today

The first Christians baptised their converts in the name of Jesus; John's baptism was a preparation for the coming kingdom and Messiah; Christian baptism was baptism into the Church of the Messiah.

Infant Baptism

A Roman Catholic baptism.

Some Churches baptise infants. Roman Catholics, Orthodox, Anglican, Lutheran, Methodist and United Reformed Churches baptise young children. The parents have to make promises to bring the child up in the Christian faith. The child can have godparents, who also make these promises. The parents and godparents have to make a confession of faith.

These are the promises and the confession of faith from the Anglican service:

Do you turn to Christ?
I turn to Christ
Do you repent of your sins?
I repent of my sins
Do you renounce evil?
I renounce evil
Do you believe and trust in God the Father, who made the world?
I believe and trust in him
Do you believe and trust in his Son, Jesus Christ, who redeemed mankind?
I believe and trust in him

Do you believe and trust in his Holy Spirit, who gives life to the people of God?
I believe and trust in him

The child is then baptised by having water poured over his or her head three times, in the name of the Father, Son, and Holy Spirit. This takes place at the font. Oil might be used to make the sign of the cross on the child's forehead, oil is a symbol of the Holy Spirit. The gift of a lighted candle might be given:

Receive this light.
This is to show that you have passed from darkness to light.
Shine as a light in the world to the glory of God the Father.

Activity

* Work out what is being said by the minister and the people in these pictures.

Orthodox Baptism

The Orthodox Churches baptise by immersing the child in the font, three times, rather than by pouring water over his or her head. The signing with oil, afterwards, is seen as very important, and it is thought to complete the act of baptism. This is called the *chrismation*.

Believer's Baptism

Other Churches refuse to baptise infants because, they say, they do not know what is happening to them, and cannot speak for themselves. They do not think that promises can be made for you; you have to make them for yourself. Baptist Churches, Pentecostal, Evangelical and New Churches baptise believers only. (They do have a dedication service, though, for infants, where the child is blessed and people give thanks for his or her birth.)

In a typical adult baptism, the candidates will be asked to give a brief testimony. This tells how they have come to find faith in Christ. The Baptist Service Book uses these words after this point:

They are here because in Jesus Christ they have found a living Lord. They have met him in a personal way, and know that Jesus, the Son of God, loves them, and that he gave himself to die for them on a cross. Each

knows that Jesus, the Son of God, was not defeated by death but was raised to life, and calls us to accept his forgiveness and hope, and to share in his resurrection life... As they go under the water and rise from it, they give witness to their desire to die to self and rise with Christ to new life.

The candidates have to answer questions about their faith, such as, 'Do you confess Jesus Christ as your Lord and Saviour?' They are taken down into a special pool (a baptistry) or they might use a local swimming pool or river, and they are pushed under the water and then pulled up again. Some women choose to wear special, long white robes.

Sometimes, the candidates shout out a confession of faith when they rise:

Candidate: Jesus is Lord!

Congregation: Hallelujah!

The Temptation
(Matthew 4:1–11; Mark 1:12–13; Luke 4:1–13)

The desert is connected with temptation and struggle against evil in the Scriptures, and in the early Christian tradition. It was the special domain of the devil, lifeless and cursed. Here, Jesus was separated from his friends and struggled with the question of his identity. After his religious experience at his baptism, he had to be sure of his mission. Three temptations are recorded, following the pattern of temptations of Old Testament heroes found in the writings of the rabbis. There might have been more, but these sum up the essence of Jesus' struggle and reveal a great deal about the kind of Messiah he believed he was. At least some of this information must have been passed on by Jesus himself, although the evangelists may have adapted it.

Stones into Bread

Jesus is tempted to turn stones into bread. This is a temptation to use magical powers to impress people into following you, without any serious thought or commitment. It is also a temptation to ignore spiritual needs and only provide material ones. Jesus replies by quoting Scripture, 'man must not depend on bread alone to sustain him, but on everything that the Lord says', (Deuteronomy 8:3).

All the Kingdoms of the World

Jesus rejects the offer to serve the devil. He is not to be a conquering king but a suffering servant who serves God alone. Much of Jesus' inspiration came from the Servant Songs in Isaiah (42:1–4; 49:1–6; 50:4–9; 52:13–53:12). Again, Jesus quoted Scripture, 'Honour the Lord your God, worship only him...' (Deuteronomy 6:13).

Putting God to the Test

The final temptation was to put God to the test; if Jesus was the Son of God, then he could throw himself off the temple pinnacle and be saved by the angels. The devil quotes Scripture here, using Psalm 91:11–12, 'God will put his angels in charge of you...' Jesus rebukes him by quoting 'Do not put the Lord your God to the test...'

Activities

Key Elements

1 Who baptised Jesus and where?

2 What relation was he to Jesus?

3 How did he dress? Why do you think the evangelists are interested in this information?

4 What happened when Jesus was baptised?

5 Why are some surprised that Jesus was baptised by John, and how do others explain this?

6 What is the difference between John's baptism and Christian baptism?

7 There are two different types of Christian baptism today, what are they?

8 How are Orthodox baptisms different?

9 What does baptism symbolise?

Think About It

10 Work in groups, and discuss whether infant or believer's baptism makes more sense to you.

11 Write a report on the three temptations, showing also how these relate to temptations in everyone's life, at times.

Assignments

12 Imagine that you are a vicar who is interviewing some parents about the baptism of their daughter. Neither of them come to Church and they do not really see the point of doing so in the future. What do you think the vicar would say? Write a short dialogue between the vicar and the parents. Work in groups on this if you wish.

13 Write a diary entry imagining that you have just been to watch the baptism of one of your friends. Describe what happens and how you feel about the experience.

Vocabulary

crib
incarnation
annunciation
Magnificat

Nunc Dimittis
Theotokos
Bar Mitzvah

minyan
baptism
believer's baptism

Lifeline Two Death and Beyond

- Questions at Caesarea Philippi
- The call of the disciples
- Women disciples and women in the Church today
- The shadow of the cross and the Transfiguration
- The Triumphal Entry into Jerusalem
- Cleansing the Temple
- The Last Supper

- The Garden and the arrest
- Trials, beatings, and Peter's denial
- Stations of the cross
- Burial and empty tomb
- Resurrection appearances
- Easter worship today
- Faith in a broken world – Alyn Haskey
- The Sadhu's story

JESUS AND HIS DISCIPLES SET OFF TOWARDS THE VILLAGE NEAR CEASAREA PHILIPPI.

TELL ME, WHO DO PEOPLE SAY THAT I AM?

SOME SAY YOU ARE JOHN THE BAPTIST, RISEN AGAIN...

OTHERS THINK YOU ARE ELIJAH, RETURNED TO PREPARE FOR THE COMING KINGDOM...

OR MAYBE YOU ARE ONE OF THE OLD PROPHETS...

WHAT ABOUT YOU? WHO DO YOU SAY I AM?

I SAY YOU ARE THE MESSIAH...

DO NOT TELL ANYONE ABOUT ME'!

This incident marked a turning point in the ministry of Jesus. Soon after his disciples confessed such faith in him, he started to return to Jerusalem, for the final time.

Extension Work

* Read through the different accounts in the Synoptics (Matthew 16:13–20; Mark 8:27–30; Luke 9:18–21). Note any differences.

The Call of the Disciples

'At once they left their nets' (Mark 1:18).

'Disciple' means 'learner' or 'student' in Greek. Jewish rabbis had, and some still have, disciples, who learn their teachings. One person reported seeing a group of Orthodox Jewish young men waiting for a car to arrive in Jerusalem. Their rabbi got out, and they surrounded him, protecting him from the crowd, and took him inside. It was a scene showing their loyalty, and it reminded viewers of Jesus and his disciples.

Jesus had a number of disciples. Luke says that there were a main group of 70 or 72 who Jesus sent out preaching (see Luke 10:1–12). All the Gospels agree, though, that Jesus chose 12 special disciples who were his closest companions. The account of their call is in Matthew 10:1–4; Mark 3:13–19; Luke 6:12–16. There are some variations in the list of names. This is probably because people had various names, they might be known by a Greek or Hebrew name. So, Simon Peter could be called by either of those names, or *Cephas*, which is the Hebrew for Peter, meaning 'Rock'. Note that in the list of the 'Twelve', there are two men called Judas, and a Simon the Patriot (or Zealot).

The Call of the Fishermen
(Matthew 4:18-22; Mark 1:14-20; Luke 5:1-11)

Matthew and Mark say that Simon and his brother Andrew were called first, followed by the sons of Zebedee, James and John. They were called when they were fishing or getting nets ready. They followed him immediately.

Luke tells a slightly different story. Jesus saw Simon and told him to push his boat out and try to catch fish one more time. He hauled in a huge catch, Simon was moved and frightened to be in the presence of a holy man. He fell on his knees and said, 'Go away from me, Lord! I am a sinful man!' The same happened for the sons of Zebedee. Then the three followed Jesus. Andrew is not mentioned.

The Call of Matthew
(Matthew 9:9–13; Mark 2:13–17: Luke 5:27–32)

Only Matthew's Gospel calls Levi 'Matthew'. He was a tax collector. Jesus saw him in his office and challenged him to follow him. Jesus went to Levi's house for a meal, with other tax collectors, and some of the Pharisees criticised him for eating with such people. Jesus replied; 'People who are well do not need a doctor, but only those who are sick. I have not come to call respectable people, but outcasts.'

Jesus probably chose 12 main disciples to represent the 12 tribes of Israel. Jesus was starting a new Israel, a revived people of God.

The Women

Mary Magdalene, from the film *Jesus Christ Superstar*, comforting Jesus before his arrest and trial.

A group of women followed Jesus and seemed to look after the domestic needs of the men. They sometimes housed them and fed them. The most outstanding woman was Mary Magdalene who had been healed by Jesus. (Magdalene meant 'from Magdala', a village in Galilee.) Luke 8:2 states that Jesus had healed Mary – seven demons had been cast out of her. This might have meant she was mentally ill, or epileptic. Traditionally, she is linked with the woman who wiped the feet of Jesus with her hair (Luke 7:36–50) who was a prostitute. This is far from certain. She supported Jesus financially, and stood by the cross (John 19:25), one of the women who visited the tomb (Mark16:1), and the first to see the risen Jesus (Mark16:9–10; John 20:11–18). The passage in John is touching and tender. There was clearly a close friendship between them.

Other women named are Mary the mother of the younger James and Joseph, Salome, Joanna, whose husband was an official in Herod's court, and Susanna. The women were at the cross when the Twelve fled.

Many have wondered why Jesus never sent any women out preaching, or included them in the Twelve. In the society of the time, it would have been very difficult for women to do that. They would have been regarded as loose women and suspect. The word of a woman carried little authority with the men of the time. (Note the reaction of the disciples to the news that the women had seen Jesus alive again in Luke 24:11; 'But the apostles thought that what the women said was nonsense'.)

Many Churches have allowed women to be ministers and preachers in this century, though the largest Churches, the Roman Catholics and the Orthodox do not. The Church of England voted to allow women to be priests in November 1992, though some other parts of the Anglican Church have had women priests since the 1970s!

Supporters of the ordination of women rejoice to hear the news that the Church of England had voted in favour of women priests.

Activities

Key Elements

1 Who were some people saying Jesus was, during his ministry?

2 Who did Peter say he was?

3 What does the word 'disciple' mean?

4 List the various groups (and numbers, in some cases) of the disciples.

5 Compare Matthew and Mark's account of the call of the first disciples to that of Luke. What is simialr and what is different?

6 What was Matthew/Levi before he became a disciple of Jesus?

7 Why do people think Jesus chose 12 disciples?

8 Why would it have been difficult to have women amongst the Twelve disciples?

9 What is said about Mary Magdalene in the Gospels? Do you think she was particularly close to Jesus?

Think About It

10 In Luke's account of the call of Peter, why do you think Peter asked Jesus to leave him alone?

11 What are your views about having women ministers/priests?

Assignment

12 Write an interview between one of the women who followed Jesus and the religious leaders of the time. She has been preaching to local people, and a number have been converted. What do you think they would say to her, and how might she reply?

The Shadow of the Cross
(Matthew 16:21–8; Mark 8:31–8; Luke 9:22–7)

Jesus warned that the Son of Man (a way of speaking about himself) must suffer. He would be rejected by the elders in Jerusalem and put to death. Three days later he would rise again. The disciples were shocked, and Peter tried to change his mind. Jesus told Peter, 'Get away from me, Satan... Your thoughts don't come from God but from man!' This is followed by the challenge to any would-be disciples – that to follow Jesus, they must take up their cross. Anyone who loses his life for the Gospel's sake will find it.

Clearly, Jesus had realised that the Kingdom of God was not going to come crashing in at any moment. He was going to have to suffer first, and then the Kingdom would dawn. Some scholars wonder how clearly Jesus would have forseen this, and they argue that Jesus only predicted suffering and then the victory of God, rather than his own death and resurrection. Others take the text as it stands, and believe that Jesus, as Son of God, would have such foreknowledge.

His challenge to the disciples was to put the Kingdom first, above their own lives, and then they would gain blessing and heaven itself. Many Christians experience a kind of inner death to selfish ways and ambitions, giving this over to God. They then feel re-made, re-born, and have a fresh view on life.

This was a turning point in the Gospel story as Jesus returned to Jerusalem, knowing that he was putting himself in the hands of his enemies.

The Transfiguration
(Matthew 17:1–8; Mark 9:2–8; Luke 9:28–36)

The Transfiguration – where the appearance of Jesus changed and shone with light – by Fra Angelico.

Jesus took Peter, James and John up a mountain to pray. He began to shine with light, and then Moses and Elijah appeared with him. They talked with him about how Jesus was going to die in Jerusalem. The disciples were overwhelmed, and Peter said, 'Master, how good it is that we are here! We will make three tents, one for you, one for Moses, and one for

Elijah!' A cloud covered them and a voice was heard, 'This is my Son, whom I have chosen – listen to him!'

Christians see this as a miracle, where Jesus revealed his divine nature. Shining, white light is used in religions to symbolise holiness. The visit of Moses and Elijah stresses that Jesus fulfilled the Hebrew Bible, being greater than Moses. Elijah was expected to return before Messiah came. The cloud was special; this was the Shekinah, an appearance of the Holy Spirit. The cloud guided the Israelites through the wilderness in the Hebrew Bible (Exodus 13:22) and rested over the Tabernacle (Exodus 40:34). The words of God echo Isaiah 42:1, as at the baptism of Jesus. The words, 'listen to him' suggest a fulfillment of Deuteronomy 18:15, where a prophet like Moses is promised, 'and you are to obey him'. The face of Moses shone with light, too, in Exodus 34:29–35, because he was in the presence of God.

Luke does not use the term 'transfigured' for this would have suggested something different to his Gentile readers. They were used to stories of gods changing shape in many ways, and the same Greek word *metamorpho* was used for these transformations as for the transfiguration of Jesus.

Some scholars wonder if this is a misplaced resurrection story (where Jesus appears to his disciples in glory). Others argue that this was to encourage both Jesus and his closest disciples before his suffering in Jerusalem.

The Triumphal Entry
(Matthew 21:1–11; Mark 11:1–11; Luke 19:28–40)

Jesus set up a theatrical entry into Jerusalem, full of symbolic meaning. He sends his disciples on to get a donkey, warning them that if people heard it was for the Master, they would let them have it. As he entered, people spread their cloaks in his path, and others waved palm branches. They sang, and shouted 'Hosanna!'

Jesus was deliberately trying to enact a prophecy in the Hebrew Bible, Zechariah 9:9:

Rejoice, rejoice, people of Zion!
Shout for joy, you people of Jerusalem!
Look, your king is coming to you!
He comes triumphant and victorious,
but humble and riding on a donkey –
on a colt, the foal of a donkey.

It was a bold statement that he was the coming Messiah, the King of the Jews. The action of the people, spreading cloaks and waving branches reflected the treatment of kings of olden days when they returned from winning great victories. 'Hosanna' meant 'Save us' or 'Set us free!' This incident made the Romans and the Jewish leaders nervous and suspicious (see Luke 19:39–40).

The use of a donkey to ride on, rather than a war horse, suggests something ironical. Jesus was to be a king of peace and not violence.

Luke omits any reference to the branches, and changes the shout of the crowd to, 'Blessed is the King that cometh... peace in heaven and glory in the highest', thus avoiding the use of 'Hosanna'. This was probably because his Gospel was for a Gentile audience, and 'Hosanna' was a Hebrew word.

Matthew quotes the prophecy from Zechariah. His Gospel often quotes verses from the Hebrew Bible, and is thought to be for a Jewish readership. It is strange that he says a donkey and a colt were taken , being too literal an interpretation of the prophecy. Hebrew poetry often used different words for the same thing in two lines of a verse.

This is how the film *Jesus Christ Superstar* portrayed the entry into Jerusalem.

Some have wondered if the crowd was staged, too, with his sympathisers greeting him as he entered the city. It is a striking scene, when the last days of his life are considered. Soon after being greeted in this way, he was carrying his own cross to the place of execution. This event was the most public statement of Messiahship recorded in the Gospels.

The musical, *Jesus Christ Superstar*, captures something of the joy and pain of this moment. The crowd sing 'Hosanna' and add 'Hey JC won't you die for me?' leaving a look of shock on the face of Jesus. This glory is going to cost him dearly.

A modern Palm Sunday procession.

Some Christians today walk around the Church, or the local streets, on Palm Sunday, the Sunday before Good Friday, carrying palm branches or crosses, singing hymns. They remember the triumphal entry of Jesus in this way. A popular modern hymn that some sing at this time is:

How lovely on the mountains are the feet
of Him
Who brings good news, good news,
Proclaiming peace, announcing news of
* happiness,*
Our God reigns, our God reigns.

Our God reigns, our God reigns,
Our God reigns, our God reigns.

The Cleansing of the Temple
(Matthew 21:12–17; Mark 11:15–19;Luke 19:45–8)

El Greco – *Christ driving the Money Changer from the Temple.*

The Court of the Gentiles in the Temple contained traders who sold animals for sacrifice or money changers who changed Gentile coins for Jewish ones. The animals had to be of the best quality if they were to be offered in the Temple, and hence the prices were high. The Gentile coins bore images of the Emperor, and were unfit to be used for offering in the Temple. The rates of exchange were also high.

This was a cause for scandal, as many Gentile visitors would have been offended by the hypocrisy. The profits went straight to the chief priests.

Jesus purged the Temple of this trade, condemning it. He re-awakened an ancient idea that the Jews were a chosen people to be a witness to the nations. The Temple was to be a house of prayer for all nations (Isaiah 56:7; Jeremiah 7:11). Mark says that Jesus drove out the traders, overturning the tables of the money changers and the stools of those who sold pigeons for sacrifice. He quoted from Isaiah and Jeremiah. Mark states that this occurred on the day after the entry into Jerusalem; Matthew

does not state what time elapsed between the two events, and his account can read as though it was the climax of the entry. Luke reads in the same way. Matthew adds that the sick came to him to be healed, and the children carried on singing 'Hosanna'.

All the Gospels state that the leaders of the Jews were determined to have Jesus killed. Matthew adds their charge to stop the children shouting. Jesus refuses and quotes Psalm 8:2, 'You have trained children and babies to offer perfect praise.'

John's Gospel places this incident at the beginning of Jesus' ministry, and this is one of the main differences in the order of events when compared with the Synoptics.

Some have wondered how many helped Jesus in the Temple; it would have probably taken more than Jesus and the Twelve. A larger group of disciples might have been involved (the 70?) and this would have disturbed the authorities as they would have feared it was the start of a an uprising.

Activities

Key Elements

1 What did Jesus say would happen when they went to Jerusalem?

2 What was the Transfiguration?

3 Why do you think Moses and Elijah appear in the Transfiguration story?

4 In what way is Jesus compared with Moses in the Transfiguration story?

5 What does the Transfiguration show about the identity of Jesus?

6 How did Jesus choose to enter Jerusalem?

7 What did the early Christians think Jesus had fulfilled from the Hebrew Bible by riding into Jerusalem?

8 Why was the manner of his entry rather 'odd' for the coming Messiah?

9 How do some Christians celebrate this event today?

10 a) Why were there money changers in the Temple?
b) What did Jesus say to them? What did he do?

Think About It

11 What do you think Jesus meant by losing your life to find it? Can you think of any examples from ordinary life?

12 Why was the entry into Jerusalem and the cleansing of the Temple a turning point in Jesus' ministry?

13 What things might Jesus 'cleanse' in the Church and in the world today if he was still on earth?

The Last Supper

(Matthew 26:26–30; Mark 14:22–6; Luke 22:14–20)

The Gospels state that Jesus sent his disciples to prepare to celebrate the Passover meal. This remembered the escape from slavery in Egypt. The meal contained symbolic foods, such as unleavened bread, bitter herbs, salt water, sweet paste , a roasted egg and a lamb bone. Some of these were eaten on the night before the Exodus from Egypt, and some were symbolic of the suffering of the Hebrews, or the joy of freedom. This was celebrated on Nisan 14 in the Jewish calendar, with a lamb being sacrificed by each family in the Temple in the afternoon.

Jesus could not have been crucified on Nisan 15, because this was a feast day and a Sabbath. Some think Jesus ate the meal on the Thursday evening (Nisan 13), after sunset, when it would have been reckoned as Friday, Nisan 14. Some Jews opted to do this if the Passover coincided with a Sabbath, and the Pharisees followed a different calendar from the Sadducees, eating the meal a day earlier. Interestingly, John says that Jesus was crucified on the day that the lambs were sacrificed.

Others have suggested it was actually a *chaburah* meal, held when friends met together.

Spencer's potrayal of the Last Supper.

These were held weekly, and Christian Communion was usually weekly in the early Church.

Jesus took bread, used so often in Jewish meals, and identified it with his body, and the wine with his blood, thus giving a way of commemorating his sacrifice. Mark 14:21 suggests that Jesus saw his death foretold in Scripture, which would have been Isaiah 53. Verse 22 states that there is to be a new covenant in his blood. There had been a covenant with Abraham, and with Moses. However, this was to be not only for the Jews, but the whole human race, as the Messiah's death atoned (made amends) for their sins.

Questions
* What happened at the Last Supper?
* What was remembered at the Passover meal?
  Expain why some Jews did not eat this meal at the same time as others.
* What new meaning did Jesus give to the bread and wine?

The Betrayal
(Matthew 26:14–16; Mark 14:10–11; Luke 22:3–6)

The Gospels state that Judas sought out the chief priests and offered to betray Jesus. They offered him 30 silver coins. (This was the amount payable for the loss of a slave in Exodus 21:32.) Matthew suggests the motive was greed, but the remorse and suicide of Judas after the crucifixion might suggest he had more complex motives. Some wonder if he wanted to force Jesus' hand into starting an armed uprising, or even into bringing the Kingdom supernaturally. 'Iscariot' might be linked to the *sicarii*, assassins who killed Romans in crowds. Then again, he might simply have been acting out of self-preservation.

Matthew records his death (27:3–10). Judas threw down the coins in the Temple and hanged himself. The chief priests, knowing it was blood money, could not put it into the Temple Treasury, so they bought a potter's field, called *Akeldama*, 'Field of blood'. Interestingly, Acts (the second part of Luke's Gospel) states that

Judas bought the field where he fell to his death – the manner of suicide being unclear (see Acts 1:18–19).

Questions
* Who betrayed Jesus, and what was he paid?
* What was this the price of?
* Why do people think he betrayed Jesus?
* What happened to the person who betrayed Jesus?

Arrest

(Matthew 26:36–56; Mark 14:32–50; Luke 22:39–53)

The garden of Gethsemane.

The garden of Gethsemane (meaning 'wine press'), outside the city, was the pre-arranged place of arrest. Jesus took his disciples there to pray, knowing that a great trial lay ahead. The disciples fell asleep, leaving Jesus praying an agonising prayer alone. 'Father, if it is possible, take this cup of suffering from me! Yet not what I want, but what you want.'

Luke's account is slightly different. There is no mention of the garden by name, or that Peter, James and John were singled out for rebuke for falling asleep. Luke adds the detail about the sweat of blood. This is known in cases of extreme anguish, and might have appealed to Luke's interest if he was a doctor, as tradition asserts.

Judas had arranged that he would hand Jesus over, knowing that he was away from the crowds in a quiet place, at night. Thus there would have been little resistance.

A kiss was a common form of greeting. The Synoptics do not say who cut off the ear of the High Priest's slave. John says it was Peter, and gives his name as Malchus. Only Luke states that Jesus healed the man. Jesus renounced the use of violence here, telling his followers to lay down their swords. Luke adds the words, 'But this is your hour to act, when the power of darkness rules', to Jesus' words about being arrested in secret, at night.

It is possible that Judas was trying to force Jesus into bringing a miraculous intervention of God at the last minute.

Denial and Trial

(Matthew 26:57–8, 69–75; Mark 14:53–4, 66–72; Luke 22:54–62. Matthew 26:59–66; Mark 14:55–64; Luke 22:66–71)

Peter followed Jesus into the courtyard of the High Priests's house, and warmed himself by a fire. He was recognised, and denied ever having known Jesus. He denied him three times, as Jesus had predicted during the Last Supper. 'I tell you that before the cock crows twice tonight, you will say three times that you do not know me.' (Mark 14:30).

Jesus was questioned before the whole Sanhedrin in the morning. Many of the people bringing charges against him could not agree. The main thrust of these seems to have been slander against the Temple, 'I will tear down this Temple which men have made, and after three days I will build one that is not made by men.' Finally, Jesus was asked, 'Are you the Messiah, the Son of the Blessed God?' (Luke just has 'Are you the Messiah?')

He replied; 'So you say' (Matthew); 'I am' (Mark); 'If I tell you, you will not believe me.' (Luke). He then added that they would see the Son of Man seated in power. In Luke they go on to ask him 'Are you, then, the Son of God?' He replies, 'You say that I am.'

This seemed to convince them of his blasphemy, which is odd, as claiming to be the Messiah was not blasphemous but slandering the Temple was.

An artist's impression of the denial of Jesus.

Questions

* Where was Jesus arrested?
* How many times did Peter deny knowing Jesus?
* Look at the painting of Peter denying Jesus. What do you think he was feeling? What do you think Jesus was feeling?
* What was Jesus accused of during his trial, and what had he actually said?
* What finally condemned him? Should this have done so?

Mocked!
(Matthew 26:67–8; Mark14:65; Luke 22:63–5)

Ecce Homo by Samantha Cary. Inset Amnesty International's symbol.

Jesus was mocked and beaten by the Roman guards. He was blindfolded and hit, and asked to play the prophet by saying who had hit him. They put a purple robe on him, suggesting majesty, and made him a crown of thorny branches.

Jesus' treatment sounds like that of so many prisoners of conscience who are beaten and humiliated simply because they have criticised their government. Amnesty International campaigns for the humane treatment and release of such people. Their symbol, a candle burning inside barbed wire, represents hope in the midst of suffering.

For Christians the mockery of Jesus was all the worse because they believe he was God incarnate.

Activity
* Find out more about the work of Amnesty International and their help for prisoners of conscience by writing to 99–119 Roseberry Avenue, LONDON, EC1R 4RE.

The Road to the Cross

(Matthew 27:32–61; Mark 15:21–47; Luke 23:26–56)

After Jesus was taken before Pilate, the Roman governor, to have the sentence of death agreed, he was led to the place of execution where he was crucified between two thieves. Victims died of suffocation as they became too exhausted to push their arms to catch their breath. A popular devotion in some Churches is the Stations of the Cross, a series of carvings or paintings of events on the way to the cross, ending with the burial. Christians stop in front of each one, they think and pray.

The Stations of the Cross.

1 Jesus is condemned to death.

2 Jesus takes up his cross.

3 Jesus falls the first time.

4 Jesus meets his mother.

5 Simon helps carry the cross.

6 Veronica wipes the face of Jesus.

7 Jesus falls a second time.

8 Jesus meets women of Jerusalem.

9 Jesus falls a third time.

10 Jesus is stripped of his clothes.

11 Jesus is nailed to the cross.

12 Jesus dies on the cross.

13 Jesus is taken down from the cross.

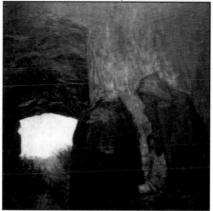
14 Jesus is laid in the tomb.

Simon of Cyrene was an African, possibly a colonial Jew, or a slave. Mark mentions his sons as they were known in the early Church. Condemned men had to carry the cross beam. Jesus was weakened by the scourging (whipping) Pilate had sentenced him to. The box in red is the only detail not found in the Gospel stories. The story of Veronica wiping the face of Jesus is a later legend, though Luke does say that women followed him, weeping.

The Last Words of Jesus

- 'Forgive them, Father! They don't know what they are doing!' (Luke 23:34)
- 'I promise you that today you will be in Paradise with me.' (Luke 23:43)
- 'My God, my God, why did you abandon me?' (Mark 15:34 cf. Psalm 22:1)
- 'Father! In your hands I place my spirit!' (Luke 23:46)

Scripture Fulfilled

Graham Sutherland's painting *The Crucifixion*.

Some of the details in the account of the crucifixion echo details in the Psalms. Psalm 22 is cry of despair from a mocked and suffering man, which fits Jesus' situation very well (see vv6–8; 16–17). The reference to the gambling to own the seamless robe of Jesus echoes Psalm 22:18, 'They gamble for my clothes and divide them among themselves.' The reference to offering drugged wine, cheap and sour like vinegar, echoed Psalm 69:21–2.

The mocking crowd misunderstood Jesus' prayer in Aramaic '*Eloi, Eloi, lema sabachthani*?' which is from Psalm 22:1, for an appeal to Elijah to save him.

The place of execution, known as *Golgotha*, or 'Place of the Skull' was, probably a rock shaped like a skull, outside the city.

The Torn Curtain

The Gospels record that the curtain in front of the Holy of Holies, in the Temple, was torn in two when Jesus died. The Holy of Holies was the place where God was supposed to dwell, and only the High priest could go in there, once a year. The tearing suggests that the way to God is open through the death of Jesus. Some think this was a historical event, and some say it was a dramatic symbol added by the evangelists to make a point. There is no definite evidence that the curtain was torn at this time, but many things from so long ago cannot be proved either way.

(One version of Josephus' history does mention that the curtain was torn, but it is not certain that Josephus actually wrote this. It might have been added by a later scribe.)

The Suffering Servant

Christ on the Cross by Mattias Grunewald.

The early Christians understood the death of Jesus as a fulfilment of a prophecy in Isaiah 53, about a suffering servant of God:

But because for our sins he was wounded,
beaten because of the evil we did.
We are healed by the punishment he suffered,
made whole by the blows he received.
All of us were like sheep that were lost,
each of us going his own way.
But the Lord made the punishment fall on him,
the punishment all of us deserved.
(Isaiah 53:5-6)

The Burial

A garden tomb.

Jesus was buried in the tomb of a wealthy man, Joseph of Arimathea. He had bought it for himself but donated it to his dead Master. Normally, bodies were taken from the crosses and burnt in the town rubbish dump, *Gehenna*. The tombs were cut into rocks in gardens, and could have a number of chambers, housing a whole family. Bodies were laid out on slabs, and a large stone was rolled over the entrance. This was very difficult to move, and deterred grave robbers. Jesus had to be buried very quickly because of the approaching Sabbath, wrapped in a linen shroud only. The women went to the tomb early on the Sunday morning to wash the body, and anoint it with the usual oils and spices, out of respect. They wondered how they would get the tomb open, but they found the stone rolled away.

The Resurrection
(Matthew 28; Mark 15:1–8; Luke 24)

The Resurrection by Piero della Francesca.

The Gospels give no actual account of the moment of Christ's rising. The soldiers guarding the tomb fell into a deep sleep, and the stone rolled away. The above painting suggests the victory of the risen Christ over the power of death.

The women found an empty tomb, with a discarded burial shroud. An angel told them Jesus was alive. They were afraid and ran back to the disciples. Mark's Gospel ends abruptly at this point (though a longer ending was added to later copies, summarising the details in the other Gospels). The disciples were hiding in an Upper Room, behind locked doors, and Jesus appeared to them. Luke stresses the bodily reality of Jesus, as he ate some fish they had. Luke also relates the story of Jesus walking with two disciples, one named Cleopas, from Jerusalem to Emmaus. They did not recognise him until he said the blessing over the bread in their house, and shared it out. Then he disappeared. The breaking of the bread sounds like a reference to the Christian Eucharist, or Communion.

Jesus is said to have risen body and soul, but his new body was not obeying the normal laws of physics. He appeared and disappeared, and walked through locked doors. The Gospel accounts suggest that the resurrection was something mysterious, but objective.

Some Christians wonder if the story of the empty tomb was added later, as a way of filling out the belief that Jesus had risen spiritually, and his presence was felt within the believer and within the Church. These Christians do not think that what happened to the body is important – it might have been stolen or left to rot. Others point out that all four Gospels have the empty tomb story, and Mark's brief account is centred around it. This suggests that it is an early tradition.

Matthew adds that Pilate ordered a story to be spread, that the disciples had stolen the body, to cover up the fact of the empty tomb.

Activities

Key Elements

1 Prepare a chart of the events from when Jesus stood before Pilate until his burial.

2 How did someone usually die of crucifixion?

3 What usually happened to the bodies of crucified people?

4 Where was Jesus buried, and why?

5 In what ways did the evangelists think the Passion of Jesus had fulfilled the Hebrew Scriptures?

6 Read Isaiah 53. What things did the early Christians associate with Jesus?

7 What was the significance of the torn curtain?

Think About It

8 Discuss in groups the last words of Jesus on the cross. What do these tell you about the sort of person he was?

Assignment

9 Imagine that you are a reporter trying to find out what happened to Jesus after his burial. You have to submit your report to the Romans. Examine the accounts of the resurrection, find any differences and similariites. Write a report, charting what was supposed to have happened. Include diagrams.

10 Design a set of Stations of the Cross, using modern photographs/drawings from magazines. Write a brief meditation at the bottom of each one. These should reflect concerns in the world about us, and link with the story of Jesus.

Easter Worship

Good Friday

Christians call the day of Christ's death 'Good Friday' because they believe that God made peace with humans, by forgiving sins through Jesus' death on the cross.

The death of Jesus is remembered in various ways. Roman Catholics and Orthodox venerate a cross, bowing, touching or kissing it as a part of the service. Roman Catholic Churches are stripped of decoration to symbolise death and sadness. The priest shows the carving or painting of the cross to the people and says; 'Behold the wood of the cross on which hung the Saviour of the world.' The story of the Passion is also read out, with several readers playing different parts.

Other Christians meet, read the Scriptures, and sing praise to God, who went to the cross in the person of Jesus. There is a note of celebration, and thankfulness for the forgiveness they feel from Jesus.

Below are words of two songs, one modern, one a traditional hymn, about Jesus' death:

Hallelujah, my Father,
For giving us your Son,
Sending Him into the world,
To be given up for men.
Knowing that we would bruise Him
And smite Him from the earth.
Hallelujah, my Father,
In his death is my birth,
Hallelujah my Father,
In His life is my life.
('Hallelujah' means 'Praise God')

The song HALLELUJAH MY FATHER by Tim Cullen
Copyright © Celebration/Thankyou Music,
 PO Box 75,
Eastbourne,
E Sussex,
BN 23 6NT.
Used by kind permission of Thankyou Music.

When I survey the wondrous cross
On which the Prince of Glory died,
My richest gain I count but loss,
And pour contempt on all my pride...

See from his head, his hands, his feet,
Sorrow and love flow mingled down:
Did e'er such love and sorrow meet,
Or thorns compose so rich a crown?

Were the whole realm of nature mine,
That were an offering far too small;
Love so amazing, so divine,
Demands my soul, my life, my all.
(Isaac Watts)

Friday veneration of the cross at Taizé.

The Taizé community in France invites young people from all over the world to spend some time in silence, worship and study. Each Friday, the cross is remembered, and people come to the centre of the church and rest their head on the painted figure of Christ on the cross. Candles are placed around this, as symbols of hope, and the belief that Jesus is alive.

Questions

* What ideas about the cross are suggested in the two hymns?
* What do you think the young people at Taizé think about the cross?

Easter Eve/Easter Sunday

Roman Catholic, Orthodox and some Anglicans, hold a special service on the Saturday evening to celebrate Jesus rising again. The evening marks the start of the third day, the day of resurrection. They light a bonfire, and a special candle is lit from this. This is the Paschal or Easter candle. It is marked with a cross, and five grains of incense are pushed into it, representing the five wounds of Jesus on the cross (to his hands, feet and side). This is carried into a dark Church as the people sing praises.

Other Christians sing praises, and read the stories of the resurrection. Some meet at dawn on Sunday morning. Most will have a service on the Sunday. Roman Catholic Churches are decorated with fresh flowers, and white cloths.

The Taizé community hold a special service every Saturday evening to celebrate the risen Jesus. A candle is lit, and thousands of small candles are lit from this in the darkened church, spreading waves of light through the crowds. Songs such as *'Surrexit Christus, alleluia, cantate Domino, alleluia!'* ('Jesus is risen, alleluia, sing to God, alleluia!') are sung.

Saturday vigil at Taizé.

> ### Question
> * Why is fire used as a symbol of the resurrection, do you think?

Easter People

Christians call themselves an Easter People. They live the way of the cross and state the power and joy of the resurrection; they know times of sorrow, but deep peace and hope from God. Two stories follow that reflect upon the suffering and the joy.

Alyn Haskey

A competitor in the London Marathon.

Alyn Haskey was born with cerebral palsy, meaning that it is very difficult to control your movements. His first sense of real achievement was when he tried for the Duke of Edinburgh's Award in his teens. At this time, he was praying 'God, if you're there, show me!' He questioned, and talked to people, and the minister at his local Church answered many of his questions and studied the Bible with him. Gradually, he came to believe, and he now speaks to people quite openly about Jesus.

Alyn has taken part in the London Marathon and the Olympics, winning a bronze medal in 1984. Many would think somone in his condition would deny the existence of God. To this he says:

If there is no God, the situation is hopeless. You can't deny there is pain, and if there is no God, there is no purpose in it. But if there is a God, there is hope... We assume that if God is love, there can be no negative things in the world. But God teaches clearly that good and evil do not cancel each other out. Jesus said, 'If you follow me, take up your cross.'...

He feels that his condition is there because nature is out of touch with God; God has not willed it. He claims that he has had a partial healing; his back is stronger, as are his legs, and he has been able to come off tranquilisers. He has also been healed of a bitterness against 'normal' people. (He sometimes wears a badge that says, 'The trouble with normal people is they don't exist!')

His faith gives him courage and strength. 'So if I wanted a prop, it would be anything but Christianity. If you're a Christian, Jesus makes demands and calls you to do things.'

Questions

* Why would the story of Jesus on the cross comfort someone like Alyn?
* What answer does he give to those who say that evil and suffering in the world suggest that there is no God?

Sadhu Sundar Singh

At the turn of the twentieth century, a 15-year-old Indian boy was in despair. His mother had died, and he was very unhappy at school. He was a Sikh, and he decided to spend the night in prayer, asking that God would show himself to him. If nothing happened, he was determined to take his own life by lying on the railway track near his home when the express came by at 5a.m.

During his time of prayer, he saw a bright light in the room. He described the scene:

In the centre there was the figure of a person. I knew at once that God had answered my prayer. The figure came towards me. I expected to see one of the Hindu gods. But no —it was Jesus! He spoke to me in my own language: 'Sundar, why do you hate me? Did I not die for you on the cross? You were praying to know the way to God. I am the way.'

I knelt down at his feet, and a great peace and joy filled my heart. Jesus had come to me in answer to my prayer. Yet he was the very last person I expected to see...

Sundar was baptised, and later became a wandering preacher, dressed as a Indian holy man, or *Sadhu*. He was lost trying to climb into Tibet, in 1929.

Extension Work

* Sundar's vision is similar to the appearances of Jesus in the Gospels. Compare this, in particular, with Saul's vision in Acts 9:1–9.

Vocabulary

disciple	*sicarii*
Transfiguration	Gethsemane
Messiah	*Golgotha*
Hosanna	resurrection

5

Who was Jesus?

- The mystery of personal identity
- The different roles of Jesus
- Son of God: a metaphor for a holy man; the King; God living as a man
- The Creeds
- Mother Teresa's response
- The Messiah, and hopes at the time of Jesus
- Did Jesus call himself the Messiah?

- Masada, the last stand!
- Jews and Christians today
- Why the first Christians believed that Jesus was the Messiah
- Modern Christians and the anointing of the Spirit
- The Son of Man: Daniel 7 and the sayings of Jesus
- Nick Beggs discovers a perfect man

Who are you?

There are many different sides to our personalities. You might be a pupil, a son or daughter, a friend of someone, and so on.

Activity

* Make a list of all the different roles you have.

The Queen, for example, is the ruling monarch, a mother, the leader of the armed forces, a grandmother and a wife.

If we ask the question, 'Who was Jesus?' we should expect a number of answers, such as:

And there are many more things that could be said by Christian believers.

THE SON OF GOD

This title is often misunderstood. Many think it means that God had a baby, that there was a physical link between God and Jesus. It does not mean this. When 'Son of God' is found in the Bible, it can mean various things.

• **A holy person who is like God** – In the East, people use the term 'son of' frequently. An insult is 'son of a camel', as camels (though useful) are smelly and spit. To be called 'son of a camel' means that you are unpleasant; it does not mean that your actual, physical father was a camel!

To be called 'son of God' meant that you were righteous, holy, full of peace and love, and, therefore, something like God. Faithful Israelites were called 'sons of God' in the Hebrew Bible. The people of Israel were called 'sons of God', as in Hosea 11.1; 'When Israel was a child, I loved him and called him out of Egypt as my son.'

Jesus once said, 'Blessed are the peacemakers for they shall be called the sons of God.'

When Christians call Jesus **the** Son of God, they mean that he was the holiest man that ever lived, a man filled with God.

• **The King of the Jews** – The Kings of Israel were sometimes called 'sons of God' in the Hebrew Scriptures. So, in Psalm 2, thought to be a coronation Psalm, v7 states: ' "I will announce," says the king, "what the Lord has declared. He said to me: 'You are my son; today I have become your father.' " ' The King was the most powerful person in Israel, and seen, in a way, as God's deputy. He had to rule the people with justice. He was like God in the power he had, hence he was 'son of God'. Jesus was sometimes called 'Son of David', for David was the greatest king of Israel mentioned in the Hebrew Bible.

The use of the title 'son of God' in the Gospels is therefore metaphorical – it stands for an idea of closeness to God.

• **God living as a man** – The title 'son of God' came to mean much, much more when applied to Jesus by the early Christians. They came to believe that Jesus was so special, and did such wonderful things, because God was in him in a unique way. They thought that the presence of God was focused in him, rather as a magnifying glass focuses the sunlight. Jesus was actually man and God at the same time; God lived in Jesus more than in anyone else. Jesus was God, living as a man.

Christianity is about God living as a man.

If you could go back in a time machine and speak to Peter before Jesus was crucified, he would probably not have thought like this. Jesus was his master, teacher, one wonderfully close to God, the expected King and many other things, but God living in the flesh? The idea had probably not even entered his head.

This belief crystalised after the belief in Jesus' resurrection. His followers thought that he must be divine if he rose from the dead. Then, all that he had said and done were seen in a new light. Why should this one man be raised in power and glory? Everyone expected to be raised up at the end of time, but Christians said that Jesus had already been raised. They saw this as God's seal of approval on everything he had said and done, proving that he was more than a man.

Examples from the Gospels

The Baptism of Jesus

The baptism of Jesus, by John the Baptist, was clearly a turning point, and an intensely religious experience for Jesus. The description of this in the Gospels has God calling Jesus 'Son': 'This is my Son, whom I love: with him I am well pleased.' This is a mixture of two verses from the Hebrew Scriptures, one from Psalm 2:7 about the king as 'son', and one from Isaiah 42:1, about a special servant of God who was sent to do his will.

Christianity is not about 'God and Son'.

It was a Jewish custom to use verses of Scripture in this way in a story to bring out the meaning. Jesus might, or might not, have heard an actual voice; but it was probably a detail inserted as a literary device by the evangelists. 'Son' here means the king, the special servant of God.

The healing of Bartimaeus

Mark 10:46–52 tells the story of blind Bartimaeus. He cried out to Jesus in the crowds, saying 'Jesus, Son of David, have mercy on me.' People tried to stop him, but he persisted. 'Son of David' was a variation on 'Son of God', meaning the king of the Jews.

The Son thanks the Father

Matthew 11:25–7 is a moving and intimate prayer of Jesus to the Father. Jesus thanks God that the good news of the Kingdom is hidden from the learned and is shown to those like children. He goes on to say 'No one knows the Son except the Father, and no one knows the Father except the Son and those to whom the Son chooses to reveal him.' This hints that Jesus used 'Son of God' in a stronger sense than just the idea of the king. He felt a special closeness with God. This helped to pave the way for the fuller meaning given to the title by the early Christians.

Activities

Key Elements

1 What does the term 'son of' mean to people in the East?

2 Which people were called 'son of God' in the Hebrew Bible?

3 What does calling Jesus **the** Son of God mean?

4 Why could the King of Israel be called 'son of God'?

5 Who did Christians think Jesus was after his resurrection?

6 Read the following passages; Psalm 2:7; Mark 1:11 and 10:46–8; Matthew 11:27. What might 'Son of God' mean in them?

Think about it

7 Have you been surprised by any of this work on the meaning of 'Son of God'?

8 Why do you think the title, 'Son of God' came to mean so much more to Christians than it had in the Hebrew Bible?

9 Look at the two pictures on p. 68. What different ideas do they give of the meaning of 'Son of God'?

God the Son

Many Christians recite a list of beliefs in their Sunday worship. This is called a creed, and in Communion services, the Nicene Creed is recited. The part that speaks of Jesus says:

We believe in one Lord, Jesus Christ,
the only Son of God,
eternally begotten of the Father,
God from God, Light from Light,
true God from true God...
of one Being with the Father...

This is affirming the belief that Jesus was God made man. Christians sometimes talk about Jesus as 'God the Son', a part of the Holy Trinity – of Father, Son and Holy Spirit. This means the part of God that lived in Jesus and revealed himself to the world. Jesus was a man, but God filled him and lived in him.

The use of the title has come a long way from the ancient meanings in the Gospels, as used by first century Jews!

Christians see this as a legitimate development though, drawing out the true significance of who Jesus was from the very beginning.

Mother Teresa

One who lives out the belief that 'God became flesh'.

Mother Teresa joined the Loreto nuns when she was 17 years old. After training in Dublin, she was sent to Calcutta, where she taught in a school for rich Indian children. She was deeply moved by the plight of the poor who were homeless, and the sick and dying who were left by the roadside. She sought permission to leave the convent to help the poor. The Pope granted permission. A family let her use a room, and she treated the sick and taught them how to read. Eventually, an old Hindu temple was given to her by the authorities, and she called this *Nirmal Hriday*, 'Place of the Pure Heart'. In 1950, she was allowed to form a new order and invite nuns to join her work. There are Homes for children, for the dying and for lepers. She tells the story of how she was given the old temple:

... the first woman I saw I myself picked up from the street. She had been half eaten by the rats and the ants. I took her to the hospital but they could not do anything for her. They only took her in because I refused to move until they accepted her. From there I went to the municipality and I asked them to give me a place where I could bring these people because on the same day I had found other people dying in the streets. The health officer... took me to the temple... It was an empty building: he asked me if I would accept it... Since then we have picked up over twenty-three thousand people from the streets of Calcutta of which about fifty percent have died.

The sisters hope that they can show a little love to the dying, perhaps the only love they have known in their lives.

First of all we want to make them feel that they are wanted, we want them to know that there are people who really love them, who really want them, at least for the few hours that they have to live, to know human and divine love.

The sisters feel that they are serving and loving Jesus in the way they look after the poor. 'Because we cannot see Christ we cannot express our love to him; but our neighbours we can always see, and we can do to them what, if we saw him, we would like to do to Christ.'

The sisters start each day with prayer, and share Holy Communion. They believe that Jesus comes to them through the bread and wine, and that he comes to them also in the poor, out in the streets. This recalls Matthew 25:40. The sisters believe that God became man, and therefore, all humans are worth helping.

THE MESSIAH

The word *Messiah* is a Hebrew word for 'Anointed One'. The Greek equivalent is *Christ*. Christ is not Jesus' surname, but a title. Jesus would have been known as Jesus Bar Joseph at the time, Jesus son of Joseph.

The idea of anointing was that holy oil was poured over the head of a king or a high priest as a symbol of God's power coming upon them so that they could do their job. It was a sign and a seal of their role. Any high priest or king of the Jews was thus a messiah, an anointed one. Gradually, the idea developed that God would send a special anointed person who would set the people free from oppression and bring peace on earth.

Hopes grew that God would send the Messiah when the Romans conquered the Jews in 63CE. There were various groups who studied the Law of Moses, and practised some kind of baptism, purifying themselves and waiting for the coming Messiah. The Qumran community, near the Dead Sea was such a group. The Dead Sea Scrolls even show they had a battle plan drawn up for when the Messiah did come.

Jar in which some Dead Sea Scrolls were found.

Ideas About the Messiah

Various ideas were around about the Messiah; many believed in a 'king Messiah'. 2 Samuel 7:14 in the Hebrew Bible was taken as a promise that such a person would come. A Psalm from the time of Jesus reads:

> See, Lord, raise up for them their king, the son of David,
> In the time which thou knowest, O God,
> To reign over Israel thy servant.

Others thought that there would be two messiahs, two anointed ones, a high priest and a king – the Dead Sea Scrolls expected this.

Another figure was known as 'the Prophet', after a promise given in Deuteronomy 18:15–18, that a prophet like Moses would come after him. Some thought this Prophet would prepare the way for the Messiah, and some believed that this would be the prophet Elijah, returning from heaven.

John the Baptist is seen as 'the Prophet' in the Gospels, preparing the way for the Messiah (cf. Matthew 3:1–4, where he dressed like Elijah). Jesus is understood as the coming king, though later, after his resurrection, the early Christians thought of him as the high priest, too, for he had opened the way to God.

Did Jesus Ever Claim to be the Messiah?

This is not clear. The most common title given to Jesus by the early Christians was 'Christ' or 'Messiah' but he never openly claimed to be this person outright. He cautioned people and asked them to be quiet when then called him 'Messiah' (see Mark 1:40–4, 8:29–30). According to Matthew, Jesus was evasive even when the high priest asked him at this trial; 'So you say', was the reply in Matthew 26:64.

Jesus' silence about the title might have been because it was a dangerous term. Anyone claiming to be the Messiah would have been closely watched by the Romans and very quickly arrested and killed. The atmosphere was electric at the time of Jesus, as many people were waiting for some sort of Messiah. The Romans were determined to stop any trouble.

Masada- a Last Stand Against the Romans

Masada is just south of the middle of the Dead Sea. This was a rick fortress in Roman times, with steep cliffs. It fell under the control of a Jewish group in 66CE. This group was called the Zealots, who were dedicated to fight to free the people from Roman control. They were zealous for the Law of Moses.

The Jews rebelled against the Romans in 66–70CE, and Masada held out until 73CE! The Zealots there all died. The last ones commited suicide rather than be taken prisoner by the Romans. Some of their skeletons have been found, clutching scrolls of Ezekiel 37, a prophecy about dry bones coming back to life. The people read this and trusted that God would raise the dead. One of their leaders, Eliazer, had urged them:

A man will see his wife violently carried off; he will hear the voice of his child crying 'Father!' when his own hands are fettered. Come! While our hands are free and can hold a sword, let them do a noble service! Let us die unenslaved by our enemies, and leave this world as free men in company with our wives and children.

Many Zealots had expected the Messiah to arrive, and God to intervene. Sadly, nothing hapened, and many suffered and died, fighting for their freedom.

Some women and children had hidden in the water conduits. When the Romans forced their way into the fortress and saw the rows of bodies, the women and children told them what had happened.

When they came upon the rows of dead bodies, they did not exalt over them as enemies but admired the nobility of their resolve, and the way in which so many had shown an utter contempt of death in carrying it out without a tremor.

The story of Masada shows the passion for freedom that the Jews had at the time of Jesus.

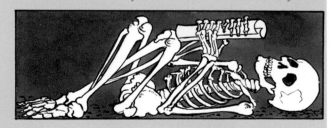

Jews and Christians Today

Many Jews still await some kind of Messiah. They believe that when he comes there will be peace on earth. A story is told about a rabbi who hears that the Messiah has come. He looks out of the window and sees a dog chasing a cat. He shrugs his shoulders and says, 'No. There is no peace on earth yet!' This is the main objection to the Christian belief that Jesus was the Messiah. He was crucified and he did not drive out the Romans. He might have been a holy man, a teacher and a healer worthy or respect, but he could not have been the Messiah.

The apostle Paul shows how scandalous the idea of a crucified Messiah was: 'we proclaim the crucified Christ, a message offensive to the Jews and nonsense to the Gentiles...' (1 Corinthians 1:23). Christians respond that God did something surprising in Jesus on the cross. He died to forgive the sins of humanity and to make peace with God. Jesus opened up a new way to God where race and tradition do not matter. Furthermore, Christians believe that

Jesus will return in glory one day, and bring the Kingdom of God to earth. So, Christians believe that Jesus has won a spiritual victory, and that one day he will bring complete peace to the world, He is to be the One who will bring peace; he is the face of the Messiah expected by the Jews.

Thankfully, Jews and Christians are on much friendlier terms, and often meet for prayer and discussion. Christians no longer accuse the Jews of being 'Christ killers', a sad term used to taunt them in the Middle Ages, and which caused many to persecute them.

Christians and Jews gather together at York Minster for a commemoration service marking the 800th anniversary of the massacre of Jews at Clifford's Tower 1190 (March 1990).

Why did the First Christians Think Jesus was the Messiah?

The Hebrew Scriptures contain many promises that a special person will be sent by God to bring peace to the people. The main idea is that there will be a king, a descendant of David who will be given great power by God. A key Scripture is 2 Samuel 7:12–15. This is a promise given to David that one of his sons will have a special mission and be blessed by God: 'I will be his father, and he will be my son.' (7:14)

▶ Micah 5:2 declares that Bethlehem will be the birth place of a mighty leader. The Gospels of Matthew and Luke state that Jesus was born in Bethlehem (though, it is interesting that Mark, John and the letters of Paul are silent about this).

▶ The Messiah would work miracles and heal people, 'The blind will be able to see, and the deaf will hear. The lame will leap and dance, and those who cannot speak will shout for joy.' (Isaiah 35:6)

▶ The Messiah would arrive in Jerusalem on a donkey, in triumph (Zechariah 9:9). Jesus entered Jerusalem on a donkey just before his arrest, clearly staging the event to recall Zechariah's prophecy.

The prophet Isaiah spoke about a child who would bring peace:

A child is born to us! A son is given to us! And he will be our ruler. He will be called 'Wonderful Counsellor', 'Mighty god', 'Eternal Father', 'Prince of Peace'...

Isaiah also spoke about a special servant of God who would bring light and salvation. 'Here is my servant whom I uphold, my chosen one in whom I delight; I will put my Spirit on him and he will bring justice to the nations.' Further on, he speaks of the suffering of this servant:

We despised him and rejected him; he endured suffering and pain... But he endured the suffering that should have been ours,... We are healed by the punishment he suffered... (Isaiah 53:3–5)

The early Christians understood this as a prediction that the Messiah would have to suffer before God's kingdom could come. Jesus seems to have used this text in this way, himself. Many Jews disagree and say that the servant in the passage is not the Messiah, but the people of Israel. It is seen as a poetic passage about their suffering throughout the ages.

Modern Christians and the Anointing of the Spirit

Many Christians today belong to the charismatic movement. This stresses the presence and power of the Holy Spirit, and special, supernatural gifts. There is lively praise, with dancing and clapping, and some people feel that the Spirit comes upon them and gives them words to say – this is the gift of prophecy. Others might speak in a special prayer language that sounds beautiful but cannot be understood ('speaking in tongues'). Others will feel that they sense the interpretation of this. Some feel

called to pray for the sick, and claim a gift of healing.

These gifts are mentioned by Paul in 1 Corinthians 12:1–11. He says 'But it is one and the same Spirit who does all this; as he wishes, he gives a different gift to each person.' (v 11) Paul lists nine gifts of the Spirit:

- wisdom
- knowledge
- faith
- healing
- miracles
- prophecy
- discernment
- speaking in tongues
- interpretation of tongues

The Holy Spirit is spoken of as giving power to each believer in the New Testament. The Greek work used is *dunamis*, similar to dynamo or dynamite. 'But when the Holy Spirit comes upon you, you will be filled with power...' (Acts 1:8)

'Charismatic' Christians at worship.

Activities

Key Elements

1 What is the Nicene Creed?

2 What is meant by Holy Trinity?

3 What two words can mean 'anointed one'?

4 What would Jesus' proper name have been at the time?

5 Describe what anointing was and what it symbolised.

6 Prophet, priest and king – describe these three ideas of the Messiah. Which was the most popular?

7 Why do people think that Jesus was wary of calling himself the Messiah?

8 Make a chart of the prophecies about the Messiah in the Hebrew Bible.

9 Read Isaiah 53 about the Suffering Servant. What different interpretations of this do Jews and Christians have?

10 a) List the gifts of the Holy Spirit and explain what they are. (See 1 Corinthians 12: 1–11.)
   b) What do some modern Christians think the anointing of the Holy Spirit does to them?

Think about it

11 Why do you think Mother Teresa and her sisters help the elderly, sick and poor? Give reasons for your answer.

12 From the evidence above, do you think Jesus thought he was the Messiah?

13 Discuss the things that would change in the world if God's peace came to it.

Assignments

14 Find out more information about the Roman siege of Masada and the lives of the Zealots hiding there. Write a small project on this, with illustrations. (If you can find a copy of Josephus' *The Jewish War*, read chapter 7, section 8.)

15 Write a debate between a rabbi and a vicar showing their different ideas about Jesus and the Messiah.

THE SON OF MAN

'AND THERE BEFORE ME WAS ONE LIKE A SON OF MAN, COMING WITH THE CLOUDS OF HEAVEN.'

'IN MY VISION AT NIGHT, I LOOKED...'

'HE APPROACHED THE ANCIENT OF DAYS AND WAS LED INTO HIS PRESENCE.'

'HE WAS GIVEN AUTHORITY, GLORY AND SOVEREIGN POWER;'

'ALL PEOPLES, NATIONS AND MEN OF EVERY LANGUAGE WORSHIPPED HIM. HIS DOMINION IS AN EVERLASTING DOMINION THAT WILL NOT PASS AWAY...'

This scene is from the Book of Daniel in the Hebrew Bible, 7:13. It is a vision of a saviour figure coming to help people. He is described as 'one like a son of man', meaning, according to the Eastern custom, 'a man'.

Jesus and the Son of Man

Jesus frequently calls himself the 'Son of Man' in the Gospels, though the title is used for Jesus only once in the rest of the New Testament! Scholars debate what he meant by it. It is striking that the Son of Man was not a common title at the time. There is no definite tradition about the Messiah using that title. Jesus seems to have made it his own, and possibly invented it.

The Heavenly 'Son of Man'

Some of his sayings probably refer to the passage in Daniel. He speaks of the Son of Man coming in power and glory:

If a person is ashamed of me and of my teaching in this godless and wicked day, then the Son of Man will be ashamed of him when he comes in the glory of his Father with the holy angels. (Mark 8:38)

Some have even wondered if Jesus was speaking of someone else here. Yet he speaks of the Kingdom coming in himself so often, that this is unlikely. He was probably speaking of himself in the future, believing that he was going to be given great power.

The Suffering 'Son of Man'

Jesus sometimes spoke about how the Son of Man had to suffer.

Then Jesus began to teach his disciples: 'The Son of Man must suffer much and be rejected by the elders, the chief priests, and the teachers of the Law. He will be put to death, but three days later he will rise to life.' (Mark 8:31)

Jesus was probably referring to the passage in Isaiah 53 about the suffering servant of God. This person is hurt and killed for the sins of the people, and then lives with God. Jesus then merged the passage in Daniel 7 with Isaiah 53. The one who was to come in glory had to suffer first. This was an original idea and an original interpretation of the Hebrew Scriptures.

A Mere Man

Others point out that the term 'son of man' appears in the Hebrew Bible meaning, simply, 'a mortal man'. So, Psalm 8 contains a meditation on the wonder of creation and how small and weak humans are within it:

…what is man, that you think of him;
mere man ['son of man' in Hebrew], that you care for him?

The title suggests weakness, frailty and mortality before the Creator. Perhaps Jesus sometimes used the term in this way, to stress that he was a servant, come in flesh and blood, and ready to die.

'Free Church' Communion.

Many modern Christians do not realise the background to the title 'Son of Man' which they read in the Gospels. Unless they have studied the Bible deeply, they are probably unaware of the idea of the heavenly saviour from Daniel. They use the title in the sense of the perfect man, or the righteous man. Sometimes, Christians talk about Jesus as 'Son of God' and 'Son of Man' in the same breath – they mean that they think he is God and man at the same time.

Finding a Perfect Man who Brought a New Start

Nick Beggs rose to fame with the group 'Kajagoogoo' in the late 1970s and early 1980s. He had been described as 'a peroxide explosion with beads' because of his hairstyle at that time! Success came with the single 'Too shy' with Limahl as lead singer. After Limahl's departure to go solo, 'Big Apple' scored a hit in 1983 with Nick as lead singer.

Nick was born in 1961, and was bored at school. His parents split up when he was 10 years old, and he lived with his mother and younger sister. 'Schoolwork was such a drag that when I left I decided that I would do something I enjoyed!' His dad bought him his first drum kit when he was 15, but at 17 he started a course in Art and Design rather than pursuing a musical career.

During this time, Nick's mother died of cancer, and he had to look after the home. He turned to drugs; 'It was a means of floating away from the realities I had to face.'

Nick was very unhappy during this period, and was searching for answers. He was living it up and hurting many people in the process. He lost friends. 'Deep down inside I didn't like myself either. I realised quite soon that what I needed was forgiveness... I wanted to wipe the slate clean and start again.'

When he started with the band, a roadie spoke to Nick about his Christian faith. He explained that Christians believe that Jesus was more than a teacher or a good man. Jesus was the perfect man, and he was God living as one of us.

> God's Son had come into the world in order to create the chance of forgiveness. Instead of us having to take the consequences... He (a perfect man in every way) took our sin upon himself.

Nick turned to Jesus, and felt that he gave him a fresh start. Nick cut out the drugs and stopped living with his girlfriends.

Nick faced criticism from the Christian world for his involvement in secular music, and one Christian magazine displayed his picture with a caption something like 'Would you invite this man to your prayer group?' Criticism came from the secular music world, too, and Nick has been involved in various projects since, fashioning his own style, but no more hits have come his way. One concern of his has been the influence of the occult in the music world. He has said ' I want to give people another option.'

In the early 1990s Nick joined a Christian group 'Iona', influenced by Celtic music and spirituality. One successful album was 'The Book of Kells'.

The group 'Iona'.

Activities

Key Elements

1 What does Daniel 7:13-14 say?

2 What does 'son of man' usually mean in Hebrew culture?

3 Why do people think Jesus used 'Son of Man' so frequently if it was not a well-known title in his day?

4 Draw a chart setting out the different senses in which Jesus might have used 'Son of Man'.

5 What do many modern Christians think when they hear 'Son of Man' read from the Gospels?

Think about it

6 Why do you think Nick Beggs was attracted to Jesus when he heard the Christian faith explained?

Assignment

7 Write down your description of a perfect man. Then think how the stories about Jesus match up to this.

Vocabulary

Son of God   anointing
creed   Son of Man
Messiah   *dunamis*

6

Jesus the Teacher

- Teaching methods
- The Lord's Prayer as a summary of Jesus' teaching
- Parables in Judaism
- Gospel parables: Lost Sheep; Lost Coin; Dragnet; Sower; Lost Son; Pharisee and

  Tax Collector; Rich Man and his Barns; Good Samaritan
- Sayings of Jesus: the Sermon on the Mount; life after death; warfare; riches
- Special actions: the Last Supper and modern Communion services

Teaching Methods

The above pictures show some of the different ways of teaching.

1 Storytelling – we hear many stories and learn things about life through them. Some of them have a moral.
2 Dictation – a teacher tells you what to write down and what to remember.
3 Discussion – teachers and pupils might talk about a subject together and think about it.
4 Visual aids – a teacher might show you a diagram to explain something.

Jesus the Teacher

Jesus used many different methods of teaching, and probably all of the above. We find stories in the Gospels, stories with a moral called parables. There are collections of his sayings, most of them short and easy to remember. He probably had his disciples learning these off by heart as other Jewish teachers of the time did. He taught them a prayer, the Lord's Prayer which his disciples memorised. He did some special actions that symbolised his message.

The Lord's Prayer

The Lord's Prayer, also known as the 'Our Father' by Christians, is a summary of the teaching of Jesus. In it, three things are emphasised:

Father

Jesus called God 'Father' more often than other teachers of his day (though others did at times!). He sometimes used a special word for God, *Abba*, that only a few Jewish holy men used. It meant 'Dear Father' or 'Dad', and was used by children for their fathers. This does not mean that Jesus taught that God was male; God is supposed to be Spirit, not having a body or a sex. Jesus meant that God was like a loving parent. Jesus sensed a close relationship with God, and wished others to enjoy this, too.

Kingdom

Jesus talked about the Kingdom of God, meaning the reign of God, a time of peace and blessing on earth. This was going to come in the future, but it could also start within people in the here and now.

Forgiveness

Jesus taught people to forgive others if they wanted God's forgiveness. God was a Father, ready to forgive, but people had to turn from their wrong-doing and receive this from God. It was no use doing a religious ritual outside, if you still hated your neighbour on the inside!

Activities

Key Elements

1 a) List the different types of teaching used by Jesus in the Gospels.
b) Which of them do you think are the most effective?

2 a) Look up the Lord's prayer in Matthew 6:9–13. Copy this out.
b) Find the parts of the Lord's Prayer which speak about God as Father, the Kingdom, and forgiveness.
c) Write a sentence explaining what Jesus meant by talking about the Father, the Kingdom and forgiveness.

Think About It

3 Discuss some situations that you think would be really hard to forgive.

Storytelling

ONCE THERE WAS A MAN...

Jesus told parables as did some other Jewish teachers of the day. The rabbis told them to illustrate their teaching, and each parable had a moral. This is the case with the parables of Jesus, though some seem to have more than one point to them.

There are parables in the Hebrew Bible too, such as Nathan's parable. King David had committed adultery and had moved the woman's husband to the frontlines in battle, where he was killed. Nathan the prophet came to the king and told him this parable:

There were two men who lived in the same town; one was rich and the other poor. The rich man had many cattle and sheep, while the poor man had only one lamb, which he had bought. He took care of it, and it grew up in his home with his children. He would feed it with some of his own food, let it drink from his cup, and hold it in his lap. The lamb was like a daughter to him. One day a visitor arrived at the rich man's home. The rich man didn't want to kill one of his own animals, he took the poor man's lamb and cooked a meal for his guest. (2 Samuel 12:1-4)

David was angry with the rich man, but Nathan pointed out, 'You are that man!' and

David was shaken and full of guilt. Why, do you think he felt guilty?

Jesus told many parables. The bulk of his teaching is taken up with them. There are parables about what God is like, about the Kingdom and about forgiveness, as well as other topics.

The picture strip below shows a Jewish parable from the Palestinian Talmud.

THERE WAS A KING WHO LOVED HIS SON VERY DEARLY.
I LOVE YOU SO MUCH, I'VE PLANTED AN ORCHARD FOR YOU...

PICK THAT FLOWER CAREFULLY AND TAKE IT TO MY SON'S GARDEN
WHENEVER HIS SON PLEASED HIM, HE SEARCHED THE WORLD FOR THE MOST BEAUTIFUL PLANTS...

BUT WHEN HIS SON UPSET HIM HE ORDERED THE PLANTS TO BE CHOPPED DOWN!

'THE KING IS LIKE GOD, WHO BRINGS BLESSINGS UPON ISRAEL WHEN THEY SERVE HIM, AND BRINGS RIGHTEOUS PEOPLE TO JOIN THEM.'

I'VE HAD ENOUGH OF THIS!
BUT WHEN ISRAEL SINS AND WORSHIPS OTHER GODS, JUDGEMENT COMES, AND THE PEOPLE ARE SCATTERED.

Moral: If you obey God, blessing and peace will come. Disobey, and things do not go right.

Activities

Key Elements

1 Imagine that you were King David hearing Nathan's parable. Discuss, in groups, what you would think.

2 What is the moral of the story from the Palestinian Talmud?

Assignment

3 Work in groups and choose a modern problem in the world. Make up some parables about this. They need not be religious.

Parables About The Nature of God

The Lost Sheep

An Eastern shepherd with his sheep.

This parable is found in Luke 15:1–7. Many people in Jesus' time earned a living as farmers. Their livestock – often sheep – were very valuable to them. Jesus told a story about a man who had a hundred sheep but lost one of them one day. He leaves the ninety-nine and searches high and low for the other one. 'When he finds it, he is so happy that he puts it on his shoulders and carries it back home. Then he calls his friends and neighbours together and says to them, "I am so happy I found my lost sheep. Let us celebrate!" ...'

> ## Questions
> * Read the parable. What does this suggest about God?
> * What moral does Jesus give this story?

Stories About the Kingdom

The Dragnet

Bringing nets ashore.

This parable is found in Matthew 13:47–50. Some fishermen cast out their net and drag it in. They catch all kinds of fish and divide the spoils between them. The worthless ones are thrown away.

> ## Questions
> * Read this parable in Luke 15. Discuss in groups what you think it means.
> * What does it suggest about God?
> * What moral does Jesus give this story?
> * Read the opening verses of the chapter, and see if you can tell why Jesus told this parable.

The Lost Coin

Luke 15:8–10 tells the parable of the lost coin. A woman has ten silver coins, but she loses one. She sweeps the house, and searches all through the house until she finds it.

> ## Questions
> * Read the parable and discuss what idea of the Kingdom is taught
> * What moral does Jesus give to the story?

The Sower

This parable is found in Matthew 13:1–9; Mark 4:1–9; Luke 8:4–8. Some seed is eaten up, some withers because it is in shallow ground, some is choked by weeds and some grows a crop into a good soil.

Jesus explanation of this parable (Matthew 13:18–23; Mark 4:13–20; Luke 8:11–15) is unusual, as he sees several points in it. It works as an allegory, with different parts of the story standing for different things. Some scholars have wondered if Jesus actually gave this exaplanation, for his parables usually have just one point. They think it might give the views of early Christians, writing them onto the lips of Jesus. The simple point meant by Jesus might have been, 'Preach the Word of God; though some who will not listen, others will.'

The dragnet tells about a time when the Kingdom will come bursting in as God ends the world to judge it. The sower tells the story of the Kingdom coming little by little, in the hearts of those who respond.

Extension Work

* Read the parable and make a chart of the different types of ground.
* Read the explanation. Discuss the meaning of this in groups.
* What idea of the Kingdom is shown by the parable of the sower?
* Retell the parable as a class and a teacher teaching. Describe the different types of pupils; some hear, others do not. Follow the outline of the original parable.

Stories About Forgiveness

The Lost Son

This parable (sometimes called the parable of the Prodigal Son) is found in Luke 15:11–32. A son takes his share of the inheritance and leaves home. He wastes his money, and ends up very poor, deserted by his friends, and feeding pigs. He returns home in disgrace, hoping that his father will take him back as a servant. When the father sees him returning, he runs out and embraces him, happy to have him back. He throws a party, saying, 'he was lost, but now he has been found'.

The Pharisee and the Tax Collector

This parable is found in Luke 18:9–14. A Pharisee prays out loud in the synagogue, when a tax collector enters and stands at a distance, ashamed of his sins and asks God for mercy. Tax collectors were hated by the Jews because they were seen as traitors. They were Jews employed by the Romans, and they often took more taxes than they should have. (Note: not all Pharisees were proud or hypocritical! Many were very devout.)

Other Stories

The Rich Man and his Barns

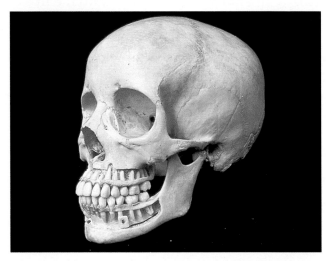

This parable is found in Luke 12:13–21. A rich man gains more and more crops, and worries about having to build bigger barns to put them in. One night, he dies, suddenly. God says to him; 'You fool! This very night you will have to give up your life; then who will get all these things you have kept for yourself?'

The Good Samaritan

ROBBER · PRIEST · SAMARITAN · LEVITE

This parable (in Luke 10:25–37) answers the question, 'Who is my neighbour?' The characters are a traveller who is robbed and beaten up, the robbers, a priest, a Levite (a helper in the Temple services), and a Samaritan. The priest and the Levite rush by and ignore the injured man, making excuses. The Samaritan stops to help, cleans his wounds with wine and oil, and takes him to an inn. The Samaritans were a race that were not trusted by the Jews at the time, so the story had a shock effect. They did not expect one to be the hero of the story!

Extension Work

* Read the parable. Discuss the excuses the priest and Levite might have had.
* Discuss why the original hearers would have been shocked to see the Samaritan helping out.
* What has this parable to say to people today who are racist?
* Write a modern version of this parable.

Some Christians use theatre to present modern versions of the parables. The Riding Lights Theatre Company, for instance, present the Good Samaritan as 'The Parable of the Good Punk Rocker' (which was more topical when first written in 1973!). In this, some football hooligans beat up a man on a train. A vicar and a social worker make excuses and do not get involved, but it is a young Punk who pulls the communication cord to get help.

The Parable of the Good Punk Rocker

NARRATOR   CHORUS…
'RHYTHM' *indicates the sound of a railway train made by the chorus with their hands slapping their thighs…*

NARRATOR: A man was on a train from London to York.
(*RHYTHM*)
CHORUS: London to York – London to York…
NARRATOR: And as he sat down to read the newspaper he fell among football fans.
CHORUS: *Football chant (clapping rather than singing)…*
NARRATOR: Who had just seen their team lose the cup.
CHORUS: BOO!! What a load of rubbish! (*Sung rather than said.*)
NARRATOR: So they mugged the man and took his wallet and his coat…

NARRATOR: Now on that train there was a vicar.
CHORUS: A—a men.
NARRATOR: Who felt sorry for the man.
CHORUS: (*Four sniffs.*)
NARRATOR So he hid in the lavatory and said a prayer…

NARRATOR: And also on that train there was a social worker…
VOICE: I really care about the kids…
NARRATOR: She cared so much about the kids that she went to the bar and had a drink…

NARRATOR: Also on the train there was the leader of a punk group called 'The Dregs'…
He was the meanest of the mean no-good guys…
But he stopped the train.
CHORUS: (*Screech. Hiss.*)
NARRATOR: 'Phoned the ambulance.
CHORUS: ('*Phoning, followed by approaching siren.*)
NARRATOR: Gave him twenty quid for a new coat.
CHORUS: (*Sympathetically*) Ahhh!
NARRATOR: And sent him off to hospital…

NARRATOR: Who was that man's real next door neighbour?
VOICE: Sir…sir…please, sir!
NARRATOR: Yes, Nigel.
VOICE: The one that did something for him!…

NARRATOR: Who showed him love…
Jesus said:
CHORUS: Go!!
NARRATOR: And do the same…

VOICE: Who is my neighbour, sir?
NARRATOR: Two, three:
CHORUS: EVERYBODY!! …

No performance of this sketch may be given without obtaining a performing licence (£10.00 for perpetuity) from 'Time to Act', c/o St Cuthbert's Centre, Peaseholme Green, York.

Sayings of Jesus

There are collections of short sayings of Jesus all over the Gospels, some contain only a few sayings, others are much longer. No one knows if he said all the sayings in a collection at the same time. They have just been remembered and put together in that way by the early Church. The longest collection of sayings is called 'The Sermon on the Mount', and is found in Matthew 5–7. Some of this material is also found in Luke 6:17-49. Matthew has this teaching taking place on a mountain, whereas Luke has Jesus coming down from a mountain and addressing the people on a plain! Scholars argue about why there are two different versions of this; perhaps Jesus taught this material to his disciples on the mountain and then came down to teach the people. Others suggest that Matthew invented the mountain, because in the Hebrew Bible, Moses received the Law on Mount Sinai, and so he had Jesus giving his new Law on a mountain. His Gospel is thought to have been written for Jews. Luke is thought to have been written for Gentiles, and so he has the action on a plain, with all the people listening. Whatever the explanation, the content of the teaching is unaffected.

The Sermon in Matthew falls into two sections; short sayings about who is happy or blessed, called the Beatitudes, and teaching on various topics. The second section can be sub-divided into: five examples from the Torah; religious duties; other sayings.

The Beatitudes
(Matthew 5:3–12)

There are eight beatitudes in Matthew, and four in Luke (where four 'woes' make up the number – cf. Luke 6:20-6). These form two line rimes in the original Aramaic language that Jesus would have used.

They are striking because they reverse the typical values of society. Happy are the poor, those who mourn, those who thirst, and so on. These have a spiritual interpretation. If people

are aware of their needs, and turn to God, seeking forgiveness and healing, then God will help them. A proud person, unable to ask for help, will receive no spiritual blessing.

Jesus also blesses those who work for peace, and those who are persecuted. The latter are blessed because they know that they are following the right path. They may be persecuted because they make others feel uncomfortable and guilty.

Note that 'happy are those who are humble' is taken from Psalm 37:11. This does not suggest weakness, but great discipline not be to aggressive. This is an attitude of listening, of patience, but of firmness.

Salt and Light
(Matthew 5:13–16)

Salt was used for keeping meat fresh, before the days of refrigeration. When it is old and damp it is useless. So a believer should keep doing good works and affect those around him or her.

Light is meant to show the way and not be hidden, and so a disciple should not keep his or her faith a secret.

There was a saying, 'The Torah is like salt.' The early Christians knew that the words of Jesus had to be like this, too.

In Judaism there was the term 'light of the world' or 'lamp of the world'. Israel was to be 'a light to the nations' (Isaiah 49:6). Jewish homes of the day were usually one-roomed, so it was possible for a lamp to light up a whole house. Jerusalem was a city set on a hill (v14).

The Law
(Matthew 5:17–20)

Jesus respects the Law of Moses and refuses to ridicule or remove any small aspect of it. However, he urges people to go beyond the righteousness of the Teachers of the Law who keep up its outward observances. It must get into people's hearts and consciences. That is most important. Christians understand Jesus as the one who fulfilled the Law of Moses by living out a life in full obedience to it, and now its details and rituals have been set aside, replaced by the law of love exemplified by Jesus. With the coming of the Messiah, the Law had served its purpose. When speaking of 'not the least point nor the smallest detail', Jesus referred to the smallest details of the Hebrew script, the *yodh* the smallest letter, and the strokes used on Hebrew letters. It is like saying 'dotting the letter "i" and crossing the letter "t" ' in modern English.

Teaching on Various Topics

Five Examples From the Torah

• **Anger** (Matthew 5:21–6) – Jesus makes the Law even harder. It is no longer enough not to commit murder, but now a person has to stop hating his or her neighbour, hence they must not call them 'Fool!' or 'Good for nothing!' (This does not mean 'fool' in the sense of likeable clown, but a term of abuse and inner hatred.) Jesus teaches that people should respect each other. He uses the term *Raca* meaning 'empty head' or 'idiot'. This insult could be tried in the local or Supreme Jewish Council. The Supreme was the Sanhedrin; the local council consisted of 13 elders.

He also talks about making peace – it is no use going through a religious ritual if you are not at peace with other people. Also, people should try to settle a dispute between themselves before going to law.

• **Adultery and Divorce** (Matthew 5:27–32) – Jesus makes the Law harder. Instead of just speaking against adultery (i.e. having sex with someone who is married to someone else) he points out that thoughts lead to actions. Lustful thoughts that seek to dominate and use people are to be avoided. Love respects and gives.

Jesus attacks a policy that made divorce very easy. There were two rival schools of rabbis, and they understood the Law of Moses differently about divorce. Deuteronomy 24:1–4 is the section of the Law in question. The Scripture talks about finding something shameful in a woman. One school of rabbis took this to mean that she had committed adultery; the other thought it meant anything that upset her husband, like burning the food! Jesus supports the former school against the latter.

• **Vows** (Matthew 5:33–7) – Jesus warns against using the name of God, heaven or any object in an oath. People should speak plainly, being honest.

This is based upon the commandment 'Do not use my name for evil purposes' (Exodus 20:7). Oaths using God's name were often used in everyday speech, or they used heaven or Jerusalem. The rabbis even distinguished between oaths that could be broken, and those that could not.

• **Revenge** (Matthew 5:38–42) – The Law of Moses had allowed retribution against an enemy, but it had carefully limited this in proportion to the crime, 'an eye for an eye, a tooth for a tooth' (cf. Exodus 21:24: Leviticus 24:20; Deuteronomy 19:21). Jesus teaches that individuals should not resist, but should shame their enemy by offering the other cheek, or by carrying something for the Romans for two miles instead of one! This is seen as one of his hardest sayings.

• **Enemies** (Matthew 5:43–8) – Jesus goes beyond the Law and teaches that people should love their enemies and pray for them. He refers to Leviticus 19:18, 34. This does not actually say 'hate your enemies', but was understood, at the time of Jesus, to mean that only fellow Jews should be loved.

Religious Duties

• **Charity, Prayer and Fasting** (Matthew 6:1–18) – Jesus warns against hypocrisy in religion, pretending to be something that you are not. Money should be given in secret, prayer should be private, and fasting personal. If people show off their piety to others by bragging about the amount they give, or making long, public prayers, or going about with ashes on their heads to show they are fasting, then they will have no spiritual reward, for they are getting their own reward by the attention they draw upon themselves.

•**Riches** (Matthew 6:19–21; 24–34) – Jesus warns about making a god out of money or possessions. He teaches that people should be rich in good deeds rather than selfish. No one can serve two masters; you have to decide which is more important to you.

•**Trust and Anxiety** (Matthew 6:25–34) – Jesus teaches that duties to God should come first, and all other things will follow on. The wild flowers he talks about are anemones that grow in Israel, and dried grass (v 30) was used for fuel. Being anxious cannot make us grow any taller or live any longer.

•**Judging Others** (Matthew 7:1–6) – Jesus warns that God will judge us as we judge others. 'Why, then, do you look at the speck in your brother's eye and pay no attention to the log in your own eye?' (v3)

• **The Golden Rule** (Matthew 7:12) – Jesus summed up the Law by saying, 'Do for others what you want them to do for you.'

Rabbi Hillel had said; 'That which you hate do not to your neighbour.' This 'golden rule' is found in other faiths, also:

Confucianism : 'What you do not wish done to yourself, do not to others.'

Buddhism: 'One should seek for others the happiness one desires for oneself.'

Islam: 'Let none of you treat your brother in a way he himself would dislike to be treated.'

HATING SOMEONE CAN LEAD TO MURDER, AND WE CAN 'KILL' SOMEONE EMOTIONALLY BY THE WORDS WE HURL AT THEM!

SOMETIMES BEING LOVING TO AN ENEMY SHAMES THEM AND STOPS THEM BEING ANGRY WITH US !

RELIGIOUS WORSHIP ONLY MEANS SOMETHING IF IT IS FROM THE HEART!

IF YOU JUDGE SOMEONE THEN BEWARE, FOR THREE FINGERS POINT BACK AT YOU!

Activities

Key Elements

1 What are the Beatitudes?

2 Where does the sermon take place in (a) Matthew, and (b) Luke?

3 Discuss two topics from the Sermon on the Mount in each of your groups, and report back your thoughts and comments.

4 What are the five examples from the Torah?

5 List all the topics where Jesus is trying to warn that wrong thoughts or motives lead to wrong actions.

Assignment

6 Write a set of Beatitudes that show the values that most people hold today, reversing the values found in those of Jesus.

Other Sayings...

Life After Death

'The men and women of this age marry, but the men and women who are worthy to rise from death and live in the age to come will not then marry. They will be like angels and cannot die. They are the sons of God, because they have risen from death.' (Luke 20:34–6)

Jesus, like some other Jews at the time, believed there would be a resurrection of the dead. (The picture above is a painting of the Resurrection by Spencer.) His own rising gives Christians hope that there is something beyond death. Read the whole episode in the Gospel, noting that the Sadducees did not believe in the resurrection of the dead.

Riches

'It is much harder for a rich person to enter the Kingdom of God than for a camel to go through the eye of a needle.' (Mark 10:25)

Jesus warns that riches can easily make people selfish and too busy to bother about God or spiritual things.

War and Peace

'All who take the sword will die by the sword.' (Matthew 26:52)

'Happy are those who work for peace; God will call them his children!' (Matthew 5:9)

Jesus warns against the waste and horror of war, and asks whether it ever really solves anything. Many question whether he was totally against war, however, and think it is right to fight against injustice.

Special Actions

The Last Supper by Emil Nolde.

Jesus used bread and wine to teach people about his death on a cross. The Last Supper was probably a Passover meal (see p. 54). Cups of wine were drunk, and unleavened bread was eaten. Jesus took a piece of bread and said, 'This is my body.' Then he took one of the cups and said, 'This is my blood which is poured out for many.' He added, 'Do this in memory of me.'

Christians have continued this custom of sharing bread and wine. They give it different names; Mass, Holy Communion, Eucharist, Breaking of Bread. Some share this every week, some a few times each month. Some use great ceremonial, with special gold or silver cups and plates. Others are informal, using an ordinary plate with a loaf, and a bottle of wine.

When Christians share the bread and wine, they are remembering the death of Jesus, and also sharing with one another. Some groups of Christians (denominations) believe that the bread and wine is transformed into the body and blood of Jesus, which is there under the appearance of bread and wine. This is called transubstantiation. The Roman Catholic Church teaches this, for example. The blessed bread and wine is bowed down to, bells are rung and sometimes sweet smelling incense is wafted before the bread and wine to honour the presence of Jesus. This belief can be seen in the prayer said by the priest when he receives the bread and wine from the people:

Blessed are you, Lord God of all creation.
Through your goodness we have this bread to offer,
which earth has given and human hands have made.
It will become for us the bread of life.

Others see the bread and wine as symbols, representing the body and blood of Jesus. All, however, believe that Jesus is present in the celebration of Communion and the sharing of the food.

This passage from the Baptist Communion service shows this very clearly:

The Table of the Lord is spread. It is for those who will come and see in broken bread and poured out wine symbols of his life shed for us on the cross and raised again on the third day. The Risen Christ is present among his people and it is here that we meet him…

This is a more modern style Communion. What strikes you about this picture?

Some modern Roman Catholics have been trying to re-interpret transubstantiation. They point out that a birthday card conveys the love of the person who sends it, and so the bread and wine convey Jesus to the worshippers. They talk about transignification, whereby the bread and wine take on a new significance, meaning, and role. They represent the body and blood.

A formal Roman Catholic Mass.

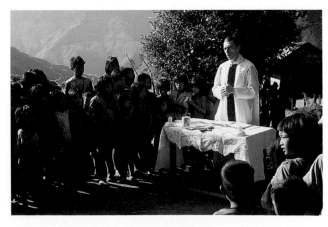

An informal Mass in the Philippines.

Activities

Key Elements

1 What did Jesus say about the bread and the wine at the Last Supper?

2 Read the different accounts of the Last Supper and note any differences that there are. (Matthew 26:26–30; Mark 14:22–6; Luke 22:14–20)

3 What different names do Christians give to the sharing of bread and wine?

4 List some of the differences in the way various groups of Christians celebrate Communion. Why do you think this is?

5 a) What is meant by transubstantiation?
   b) What is meant by transignification?

c) How do other Christians understand Communion?

6 Read through this prayer from the end of an Anglican Communion service:

Almighty God, we thank you for feeding us with the body and blood of your Son Jesus Christ.
Through him we offer you our souls and bodies to be a living sacrifice. Send us out in the power of your Spirit to live and work to your praise and glory. Amen.

What beliefs about Communion can you find here? What benefits do the worshippers seek from it?

Think About It

7 Jesus was using a visual aid when he taught people to share bread and wine. What was the point of it? Do you think this is an effective way of teaching?

8 If possible, attend a Christian Communion service and observe what is happening. What feelings do you have there? What message is being given?

Vocabulary

Parable
transubstantiation
beatitudes
transignification

Communion
Eucharist
Mass
Levite

7

The Kingdom

- The sermon at Nazareth
- Teaching about the Kingdom
- Parables of growth
- Parables of discovery
- Parables of the coming Kingdom

- What are miracles?
- Nature miracles and healing miracles
- Modern healing miracles
- Base Communities and Liberation Theology

JESUS WENT TO A SYNAGOGUE IN NAZARETH, WHERE HE HAD BEEN BROUGHT UP. HE STOOD UP TO READ FROM THE SCRIPTURES.

HE FOUND THE PLACE IN THE BOOK OF ISAIAH WHERE IT IS WRITTEN:

THE SPIRIT OF THE LORD IS UPON ME, BECAUSE HE HAS CHOSEN ME TO BRING GOOD NEWS TO THE POOR...

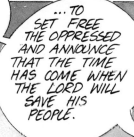

HE HAS SENT ME TO PROCLAIM LIBERTY TO THE CAPTIVES AND RECOVERY OF SIGHT TO THE BLIND;

...TO SET FREE THE OPPRESSED AND ANNOUNCE THAT THE TIME HAS COME WHEN THE LORD WILL SAVE HIS PEOPLE.

THIS PASSAGE OF SCRIPTURE HAS COME TRUE TODAY AS YOU HEARD IT READ.

ISN'T THAT YOSIF'S SON?

WHO DOES HE THINK HE IS?

Activity

* Read the passage in Luke 4:16–30. How do the people respond to what Jesus says?

Jesus and the Kingdom of God

Jesus taught a great deal about the Kingdom of God – a time of peace and blessing on earth, when evil would be judged, and suffering cease. Many Jews longed for a new age when Israel would be liberated from the Romans. Mark's Gospel makes the preaching of the Kingdom central to Jesus' message from the beginning: Mark 1:15, ' "The right time has come," he said, "and the Kingdom of God is near! Turn away from your sins and believe the Good News!" '

Jesus taught that the Kingdom would come suddenly, by the power of God. He also taught that it would grow gradually, inside people.

Rodney Matthew's painting of the Enthroned Christ.

Mark 13 contains Jesus' teaching about the end of the world and the coming Kingdom. He describes a time of battles and persecution of his followers (vv5–13). He also warns that many will come claiming to be the Messiah.

In vv14–23 he speaks of a calamity that is to come upon Judaea, and of 'The Awful Horror', which probably meant the setting up of a pagan idol in the Holy Place of the Temple in Jerusalem.

In vv24–31 he describes the sign of the Son of Man, understood as his appearance in glory to judge the world. 'Then the Son of Man will appear, coming in the clouds with great power and glory. He will send the angels out to the four corners of the earth to gather God's chosen people from one end of the world to the other.' He tells people to watch for warning signs, just as when you see a fig tree putting out leaves, you know that summer is approaching. He seems to claim that none of those listening to him will die before the end comes (v30), but this could be interpreted as those who are alive in the days that he is predicting.

In vv32–7, Jesus is careful to warn people that no one can work out when the time will come, and he warns them to be alert. He tells the parable of the master of the house going on a journey. He returns by surpirse, and catches his doorkeeper asleep. Matthew 24:36–42 adds some details to this section; some people will be taken, some left behind to face judgement. Jesus compares the coming of the kingdom with a thief coming by surprise in the night.

Parables of the Kingdom

Hidden Growth

Some of the parables suggest that the Kingdom is already present, growing in secret.

•**The Seed growing in secret** (Mark 4:26–9) – When Jesus actually told this, he probably expected that the harvest would come very soon, as he was present as Messiah. The seed had been growing throughout the history of the people of Israel.

When the early Christians interpreted this parable, they applied it to the period between the Ascension of Jesus and his *Parousia* (Second Coming).

• **The Mustard Seed** (Matthew 13:31–2; Mark 4:30–2; Luke 13:18–19) – This is about speedy growth, using a Jewish proverb, 'Small as a grain of mustard seed.' Faith would bring a rapid building of the Kingdom. Jesus probably meant that the kingdom was already present, in him, for all those who wished to shelter under its protection (cf. Daniel 4:12). For the early Christians, the rapid spread of the Gospel and the many converts were the tree growing from so small a seed – Jesus, the Twelve, and some other followers.

• **The Leaven** (Matthew 13:33; Luke 13:20–1) – Leaven, or yeast, is a transforming influence, making dough rise. So, the influence of the Gospel is a leaven transforming society. This applied to Judaism in the time of Jesus, but the early Church saw this as a power at work all over the world.

• **The Tares** (Matthew 13:24–30, 36–43) – This is like the seed growing secretly. Good and bad influences are at work together. At the time of the harvest, the tares will be sifted out and destroyed.

Jesus probably applied this to the history of Israel. Some think that vv36–43 are not part of the original parable, but were added as an interpretation by the early Church. These verses see this parable as applying to the period between the Ascension and the Parousia. Of course, Jesus might have foreseen that the Kingdom would have been delayed.

Note that some of these parables have a last judgement, and a return of Christ. To say that the Kingdom is already present does not rule out its coming in fullness one day.

Parables of Discovery

• **The Hidden Treasure** (Matthew 13:44)
• **The Pearl of Great Price** (Matthew 13:45–6)
These two parables are about a joyful discovery. The items are so precious that people sell all they have to get them. The parables suggest that the Kingdom is already present, waiting to be found by all those whose hearts are ready.

Parables About the Coming Kingdom

• **The Great Supper** (Luke 14:15–24)
• **The Marriage Feast** (Matthew 22:1–10)
These might be variations on the same story. The Messianic kingdom was often symbolised by a great banquet or wedding feast. All are invited, whatever rank in society. This was probably addressed to the Jews by Jesus, but was seen to include the Gentiles by the early Church. The end of the Wedding Feast speaks about the wedding garment (some think this might have been part of an originally separate parable). This reflects a parable told by the rabbis about some being dressed ready for the banquet, and some not. To be dressed ready for Jesus, would have meant responding to his call while there was time.

A Jewish wedding feast.

• **The Labourers in the Vineyard** (Matthew 20:1–16) – A Roman denarius, was the coin paid to workers in the fields for a day's labour. A generous employer would pay a full denarius for someone hired late in the day, who had been waiting, looking for work.

Jesus told this parable to stress the generosity of God. The Kingdom was going to be open to all who heard, even at the last minute. A vineyard had been a symbol of Israel in the Hebrew Bible. The early Christians saw the late comers as Gentiles, who were given the same blessings as the people of Israel.

• **The Ten Virgins** (Matthew 25:1–13) – The scene is an Eastern wedding when the bridegroom would come from much feasting to claim his bride and take her home. It is not clear if the virgins are waiting at the bride's house, or the bridegroom's. Some suggest they might have been male servants, rather than women.

This is a parable about watchfulness; waiting for the coming of the Kingdom. The early Church saw this as a parable about preparing for the Parousia; 'Be on your guard, then, because you do not know the day or the hour.'

• **The Sheep and the Goats** (Matthew 25:31–46) – This was told about the coming of the Son of Man in judgement. Jesus was probably speaking about his own appearance in glory to judge the nations. The people are separated into sheep on the right, and goats on the left. In the East, the right side is associated with goodness and blessing, and the left with cursing. The sheep are easy to control and obey the master's voice. The goats are self-willed and disobedient.

Some of the sheep are surprised to be counted as sheep, 'When did we ever see you a stranger and welcome you into our homes?' Likewise, some of the goats are surprised too! Jesus shows that people will be judged on their inner motives; only God knows people's hearts.

Some see this as implying that members of other faiths or even atheists who seek truth and compassion and live by them, will be given a place in the Kingdom.

Miracles

The miracles of Jesus are seen as signs of the Kingdom in the Gospels. Matthew 11:1–6 tells how some disciples of John the Baptist came to

Jesus asking, 'are you the one John was expecting to come, or should we expect someone else?' Jesus replied; 'the blind can see, the lame can walk, those who suffer from dreaded skin-diseases are made clean, the deaf hear...' that is his answer.

What is a miracle?

A miracle is a wonderful event that we cannot explain scientifically. Water turned into wine; a virgin birth; rising from the dead; a person prayed for who gets better suddenly.

If such things happen, then they might be the power of God at work which human beings can never understand. The normal laws of nature are set aside by their Creator, who gets involved in the world in a direct way.

Others suggest that God works through the laws of his creation, rather than interfering with them. Only, there are laws that science has not yet discovered. Imagine going back in time a few hundred years and trying to tell people about electric light bulbs! They would see it as magic.

Some scientists are interested in the idea of 'mind over matter', and have done experiments with hypnosis. Hypnotised people are told that hot metal is touching them when it is actually cold. Their skin blisters! There is a great deal about the human brain and the power of the mind that we do not yet understand. We do know that many sicknesses are connected with our feelings; worry can produce headaches, back pain, and sickness, for example. Guilt can cause many problems.

Mark 2:1–12 tells the story of the healing of a paralysed man. The healing only happened after Jesus told him he was forgiven. Was this man ill because of his guilt?

Others call any amazing, wonderful events miracles, even if we can explain them, like the beauty of a sunset, dew glistening on a spider's web, or a baby's first smile!

Nature Miracles and Healing Miracles

Nature miracles are where Jesus changes something in the world around him; he calms a storm, or walks on water. Healing miracles affect people only. There are many types of healings in the Gospels, and only a few nature miracles. Some scholars have suggested that, while Jesus really did heal people, the nature miracles are like parables. They are made up stories with a meaning. Some Christians do not agree with this. They would rather see the nature miracles as examples of the power of God working in his creation through Jesus.

Two Nature Miracles

•**Jesus walks on the water** (Mark 6:45–52; Matthew 14:22–33) – Many see this as a genuine miracle, showing the power of God over creation. Others have wondered if the evangelists were mistaken. Perhaps Jesus was only walking by the edge of the sea. The Greek preposition for 'on' can mean 'by', or 'next to'.

Others argue that this was made up by the evangelists. Water is often a symbol for chaos and evil in the Hebrew Bible. The story of creation in Genesis 1 has God's Spirit moving over the raging waters, bringing order out of chaos. Perhaps the story of Jesus on the water suggested that he had overcome evil, and it was written to help the early Christians who were suffering for their faith.

It is possible, though, that the event happened to make a symbolic point. A miracle can have a moral, even if it really happened. Note that Matthew adds that Peter tried to follow Jesus by walking on the water, when he became afraid, he started to sink.

•**Feeding the 5,000** (Mark 6:30–44; Matthew 14:13–21; Luke 9:10–17) – Jesus takes five loaves and two fishes that the disciples had found, and blesses them. The crowd of 5,000 is fed as these are passed round, and the disciples gather up 12 baskets filled with scraps.

This is often seen as the power of God at work, multiplying the food. Others see this as a story about sharing, and see the miracle as taking place in a very different way. Perhaps, they say, the people had food on them, hidden away, because they did not want to share it with so many. The example of the disciples, sharing what little they had, made them share, and there was more than enough for everyone.

The Gospels do not actually say it was a miracle, but it was probably understood to be. The prophet Elisha had fed a large number in a similar way (2 Kings 4:42–4). The Messiah would have been expected to do something similar. The evangelists might have misunderstood the event themselves, and have been influenced by the story in the Hebrew Bible.

Note that Mark 8:1–10 and Matthew 15:32–9 has a second feeding miracle, when 4,000 are fed. Some see this as a doublet, where one miracle story is repeated. Mark might have had two versions of the same incident, and thought they were two separate ones. Others argue that Jesus did this miracle on two separate occasions.

Healing Miracles

•**Daughters of Israel** (Mark 5:21–43; Matthew 9:18–26; Luke 8: 40–56) – One story presents two miracle stories in one, the healing of an old woman, and the raising up of a young girl.

'If only I touch his cloak' (Matthew 9:21).

The old woman had suffered from internal bleeding for many years, and would have been weakened by this. She reached out in the crowd and touched Jesus' robe. Luke says that Jesus felt power go out from him. He blessed the woman and she was cured.

This was on a journey to visit the recently deceased daughter of Jairus, a Jewish official. When the party arrived at the house, there were mourners weeping and wailing, as was the custom. Jesus declared, 'Get out everybody! The little girl is not dead – she is only sleeping!' The crowd laughed at him, but they left. He took the girl by the hand . Mark has Jesus saying, '*Talitha koum*', which means 'Little girl, I tell you to get up!' (*Talitha* actually means 'little lamb' in Aramaic.)

For the early Christians, this story showed the power of Jesus over death, and this foreshadowed his own resurrection. Some have wondered if the girl was in a coma, and Jesus knew this, hence saying that she was sleeping. This expression probably meant that she was dead though, for the dead slept until Messiah came and the resurrection at the end of the age.

A similar raising story can be found in Luke 7:11–17, the raising of the widow of Nain's son.

The Raising of Jairus's Daughter, a painting by Jacomb Hood.

•**The madman in the tombs** (Mark 5:1–20 Matthew 8:28–34; Luke 8:26–39) – Jesus was an exorcist as well as a healer. People believed in evil spirits, and saw these as fallen angels, afflicting human beings in many ways. An exorcism set someone free from demonic influence. One story is of the Gerasene Demoniac.

He was an uncontrollable outcast who wandered in the tombs, cutting himself and breaking free of any chains put on him. He fell at the feet of Jesus and begged to be set free. He claimed that his name was 'Legion', or 'Mob', because he believed that so many demons were inside him. Jesus set him free, and the spirits asked permission to be sent into a herd of pigs nearby. They ran over the edge of the cliff. People were amazed to see the man clothed and in his right mind.

(People believed that the demons would be chained up in a pit until the day of judgement, and hence their wish to go into the pigs. Pork was an unclean meat for the Jews.)

This story raises a number of issues. Some modern Christians do not believe in evil spirits. They think these were old-fashioned ways of speaking about mental illness, and compulsions that drive people to do destructive things. Jesus healed the man's mind, in the story, but did not drive out any actual devils. The herd of pigs were probably frightened by the screams of the man.

Other Christians disagree. They say evil spirits are just as real today, pointing to stories of people who are prayed for and who throw themselves across the room, speak in a voice that is not their own, or have unnatural strength. These people say they feel something leave them, and they feel a deep peace afterwards. The pigs in the story might have been just scared, or Jesus might have given permission for the spirits to enter them because he knew he was dealing with a very great evil power, and this would have made things safer for those around.

JESUS THE NAZARENE HEALS THE SICK!

A Syro-Phoenician woman told us that her daughter is completely well. She had been troubled, restless, and out of control. Many believed she had a demon in her. Though a non-Jew, this woman approached Jesus and begged him to help. When he showed surprise that a non-Jew came to him, she said, 'Even the dogs under the tables eat their master's left-overs!' He praised her faith as being greater than that found in Israel, and spoke a word of healing for her daughter (who was not present.) When the woman returned home, she found her daughter cured.

The final story in this report is of a man cured of an awful skin-disease. He has presented himself to the Temple priests who have pronounced him cured and clean. He was one of a group of ten who asked Jesus to heal them. He did so, but this man was the only one to return and show gratitude. He was a Samaritan! Jesus said to him; 'There were ten men who were healed; where are the other nine? Why is this foreigner the only one who came back to give thanks to God? Get up and go; your faith has made you well.'

Another surprising story comes from a Roman centurion, who is friendly to the Jews and has contributed to the building of a synagogue. His servant was ill and dying. He begged Jesus to help, and he spoke a word of healing. Again, he returned to find the servant cured. He came out to find Jesus, believing that he was not worthy to have him in his house.

These three stories can be found in Mark 7:24–30; Luke 7:1–10; Luke 17:11–19.
They are striking because they show the compassion of Jesus for non-Jews – a Phoenician, a Roman and a Samaritan. (Though there are many stories of his fellow Jews being healed, such as Blind Bartimaeus - see p. 69.)
The ten lepers probably did not suffer from what we call leprosy today, but another type of infectious skin disease, which made them outcasts, having to live in special areas.

Activities

Key Elements

1   What ideas about the Kingdom of God are present in the parables of Jesus?

2   What different understandings of the 'word' miracle are there?

3   Write a sentence to define (a) a nature miracle (b) a healing miracle and (c) an exorcism.

4   Describe one example of a nature miracle.

5   Take one healing miracle and find out the following information:

   •What was the problem?
   •Who approached Jesus?
   •How did Jesus respond?
   •What happened as a result?

Think About It

6   How might the nature miracle you have chosen in 4 above be explained today? Would you be convinced by this?

7   Some of the healing miracles might also be explained by modern science. Explain how this might be done.

8   Discuss in groups about belief in miracles.

Modern Stories of Healing

A Visit to Lourdes

At Lourdes, a Roman Catholic shrine in France, a young girl, Bernardette, is said to have had a vision of the Virgin Mary in the nineteenth century. A spring appeared, and pilgrims go to pray, to receive Communion, and to bathe in the spring waters. Many people say their condition improves as a result, but the Church employs a team of doctors who check out any claim of healing. They are very strict and thorough. They only accept a cure as a miracle if it is complete and occurs suddenly, when there was little or no hope of any improvement through time or medicines. Less than a hundred

Pilgrims visiting the shrine at Lourdes.

cases have been accepted since the shrine opened. This is one person's story.

Jeanne Fretel suffered from a serious illness for ten years and had had unsuccesful operations. She had to have three to four injections of morphia a day because of pain, high temperature, vomiting and a swollen abdomen. She was taken to Lourdes in a semi-conscious state in 1948. She was not aware she was being taken taken there. She went to Mass, and the baths, but there was no improvement until the Friday. She was taken up to the altar and the priest gave her a small part of the host at Communion, as she was dying. This is what she felt:

Then I suddenly felt well and realised that I was at Lourdes. I was asked how I felt. I said I felt well. My stomach was still hard and swollen but I no longer suffered at all. I was given a cup of cafe-au-lait. I had regained my appetite. I was able to keep it down... [At the grotto] I felt as though someone took me under my arms to help me to sit up. Then I found myself in a sitting posiiton. I turned around to see who could have helped me, but I couldn't see anyone. As soon as I sat up, I felt the same hands which had already helped me take my own hands and put them on my stomach. I first wondered what had happened. Was I cured, or was I dreaming? I noticed that my stomach had become normal.

Further tests followed, checking for abdominal pain and swelling, the symptoms had disappeared and twenty doctors signed a statement that her illness had gone.

Jennifer Rees Larcombe – An Unexpected Healing

Jennifer suddenly became ill in 1982. She was taken into hospital in Kent, diagnosed as suffering from encephalitis. This is an inflammation of the brain and the membranes surrounding it, usually caused by a viral infection. Jennifer was in great pain, and could not walk. She became dependent on other people, and found this very humiliating. Her family of seven rallied round and supported her. Eventually, she was allowed home but in a wheelchair.

She was speaking at a meeting at a Church group in Haselmere, Surrey, when a young woman spoke from the back of the meeting. 'I've never had anything like this happen to me before. I've only been coming to church for a few months, you see. But I feel God is telling me to tell you that you are going to get well.'

She was so nervous, that she tried to leave the meeting, but Jennifer asked her to pray for her. She did not feel able to do that, and left. She went to find one of the leaders, but he sent her back. 'You have been given this conviction, so you must pray.'

Someone told the woman, called Wendy, to place her hands on Jennifer, and 'Just allow God to use your hands as you pray, then his power can flow through them.'

Jennifer describes what happened next:

I felt absolutely nothing. No sensations nor even any emotion. Just a matter-of-fact satisfaction of knowing a job had been done at long last.

When I opened my eyes no one gazed at me to see if I would stand up, because no one really expected that I would – except Wendy.

'Well', I said when people began to drift away, 'I'm not going out of here in a wheelchair.' The moment I moved, I knew there was something different...

Rigid muscles loosened, and she was able to walk. She was so embarrassed that she went straight to the toilet and practised moving her limbs in private!

Jennifer before she was healed.

Jennifer with her husband after she was healed.

The Kingdom Today

A meeting at a base community.

While wonderful stories like this do seem to happen, other people with illness or disability are prayed for and do not recover so miraculously. This is a mystery for Christians. One woman with a curved spine, wrote about Christian preachers who speak of 'the bondage of a wheelchair':

For many people, their wheelchair is their lifeline, their key to mobility, you can't just dismiss them and encourage people to walk instead. How can you pray triumphalistically for people to be healed from deafness and yet claim to respect deaf people as equal human beings? Whose is the problem here?

I certainly have been prayed for by people who actually had far more of a problem with my curved spine than I do... (Michelle Taylor, in *Alpha* magazine, January 1993.)

Some people seem to be healed, but it is a far from perfect world, and the sick need compassion and understanding.

Extension Work

* Write an imaginary diary entry for either of the people above after they were healed.
* Write down some comments by a disabled person after reading a magazine article about someone who is healed.

Many Christians are working for justice in the world. Each improvement, each person helped, is a little bit more of the Kingdom brought into the world. In Latin America, a large number of priests and people are involved in Liberation Theology. Theology means 'thoughts about God' and liberation means 'freedom'. Liberation Theology means that thoughts about God should help to set people free.

In Latin America, there is a great divide between rich and poor. Rather than build ornate cathedrals and churches, many priests live and work in blocks of flats or the shanty towns. They help form 'base communities' where ordinary people are trained as teachers and co-ordinators. They hold prayer meetings, teach the Bible, and apply this to their needs. They protest and petition the government. For example, one base community protested that a school had been closed down because the drains were blocked. The authorites came and unblocked them!

There can be suffering. Archbishop Romero of El Salvador was shot during Mass for his outspoken sermons against the government. He also supported the base community movement. In one area of San Salvador, the capital, he refused to divide up a new housing estate into parishes, and let five priests live in the flats. Base communities were formed in different flats. Some of the priests were expelled by the government, and one was shot.

Oscar Romero, assassinated in 1980.

Father Rutilio Grande was another priest working in El Salvador. He came to the town of Aguilares in 1972 with a team of Jesuit priests. There he worked for the poor and preached fiery sermons. Rutilio delighted in telling people, 'God is not somewhere up in the clouds lying in a hammock. God is here with us, building up a kingdom here on earth.' He once preached against the government, comparing the people of the country to Cain and Abel in the Bible. Just as Cain killed his brother Abel, so the rich are killing the poor.

> You are the Cains, and you crucify the Lord in the person of Manuel, of Luis, of Chavela, of the humble campesino. There are those… who would prefer… Christ, a dummy to be carried through the streets in processions, a Christ with a muzzle in his mouth, a Christ made to the specifications of our whims and according to our own petty interests. They do not want a God who will question us and trouble our consciences, a God who cries out: 'Cain! What have you done to your brother Abel?'…

On Saturday 12 March 1977, Rutilio was shot when travelling by jeep to say Mass.

A modern hymn, 'God's Spirit is in my heart' by Alan Dale and H.J. Richard's, sums up all these hopes and feelings of trying to build the Kingdom:

> God's Spirit is in my heart.
> He has called me and set me apart.
> This is what I have to do.
> What I have to do.
>
> He sent me to give the Good News to the poor,
> tell prisoners that they are prisoners no more,
> tell blind people that they can see,
> and set the down trodden free,
> and go tell ev'ryone the news
> that the Kingdom of God has come,
> and go tell ev'ryone the news
> that God's kingdom has come.

Extension Work
* Design a poster showing the activities of a typical base community.
* Find out more information about Bishop Oscar Romero.

Vocabulary

base communities
exorcism
Liberation Theology
miracle
Parousia

8

Conflict

- Jesus before Pilate
- Jesus tried by Annas and Caiaphas
- Why the Romans were against Jesus
- Why some of the groups in Judaism opposed Jesus
- Conflict stories: debating with the Sadducees; questioning tradition; eating with sinners; Zacchaeus; Mary and Martha; the Phoenicean woman
- Jesus, non-violence and warfare
- The story of Ken Lancaster

Behold the Man!

In this painting, Pilate shows Christ to the crowd. 'Behold the man!' he says. There was a custom of releasing one prisoner at Passover time, to appease the Jews. Jesus was offered along with Barabbas, a freedom fighter. The crowd chant for Barabbas and Pilate is surprised.

Questions

* What emotions are going on in the picture? How is Jesus feeling? What about Pilate? How is the crowd feeling?

Pilate was a Roman ruler well able to deal with criminals. The meek, quiet Jesus was not what he was used to. Freedom fighters and self-styled Messiahs would curse and swear at him. This man stood silently before him. The Gospels suggest that Pilate was unnerved by Jesus. He hoped the scourging would keep the crowd happy.

The Gospels tell the story in Matthew 27:1–2, 11–26; Mark 15:1–15; Luke 23:1–5, 13–25. Matthew adds the detail (v 19) that Pilate's wife sent him a message; 'Have nothing to do with that innocent man, because in a dream last night I suffered much on account of him.' Pilate off loads the blame onto the crowd and says he washes his hands of the affair.

Pilate was known to be a ruthless man. A Jewish writer, Philo of Alexandria, describes him thus; 'He was cruel and his hard heart knew no compassion. His day in Judaea was a reign of bribery and violence...'

The historian Josephus says that Pilate upset the Jews as soon as he arrived. He ordered the Roman troops to march into Jeruslam with their standards that bore the image of the Emperor. The Jews objected to this, and protested. Jospehus says what happened next;

The next day Pilate took his seat on the tribunal in the great stadium and summoned the mob on the pretext that he was ready to give them an answer. Instead he gave a pre-arranged signal to the soldiers to surround the Jews in full armour, and the troops formed a ring, three deep. The Jews were dumbfounded at the unexpected sight, but Pilate, declaring that he would cut them to pieces unless they accepted the images of Caesar, nodded to the soldiers to bare their swords. At this the Jews as though by agreement fell to the ground in a body and bent their necks, shouting that they were ready to be killed rather than transgress the Law. Amazed at the intensity of their religious fervour, Pilate ordered the standards to be removed from Jerusalem forthwith.

Pilate (for once) backed down!

The musical, *Jesus Christ Superstar*, focuses upon the idea of Pilate being disturbed by the presence of Jesus. We see Pilate confused and troubled before the trial. The song 'Pilate's Dream' opens with,

I dreamed I met a Galilean.
A most amazing man.
He had a look you very rarely find,
the haunting, hunted kind.

It ends with,

Then I saw thousands of millions
crying for this man.
And then I heard them mentioning my name
And leaving me the blame!

Why Would the Romans Want to Kill Jesus?

Although the Synoptics give the impression that the Romans only tried Jesus reluctantly, at the end of his career, it is highly likely that they were watching the preacher from Nazareth all though his public ministry. Galilee was a notorious place for rebels; Judas the Galilean had led an uprising in 6CE and thousands had been crucified as a result. Anyone preaching the coming of a new kingdom would have been under immediate suspicion, for it was a challenge to the rule of Rome. Any claim to be the Messiah was dangerous; you would be branded a trouble maker and would-be king of the Jews. John, the fourth Gospel, hints that the Romans were much more closely involved. In the account of the arrest in the Garden of Gethsemane, it says; 'So Judas went to the garden, taking with him a group of Roman soldiers, and some temple guards sent by the chief priests and the Pharisees.' (John 18:3)

According to the Gospels, Pilate's hand was forced by the plea that if Jesus called himself a king, then he must be an enemy of Rome, though Jesus seemed to be more a holy man rather than a political revolutionary.

Jewish Opposition

The Sadducees were the main Jewish group to oppose Jesus. He preached a coming Kingdom. This challenged the delicate status quo that had been negotiated with the Romans. Jesus also preached the resurrection, which they rejected.

Jesus was closer to the Pharisees, though there are passages where he seems to dismiss them as hypocrites. They also preached the resurrection, and a coming Kingdom.

The Zealots, who were prepared to take up arms againt Rome, would have warmed to the idea of a coming Kingdom, but they would have grown disillusioned with Jesus' use of non-violence. ('Zealot' is used in this chapter for anyone prepared to fight against Rome.)

Most of the Jewish groups would have been offended by Jesus' attitude to the Temple.

The incident of the cleansing of the Temple, though meant to be an act of profound respect and purification ('My temple will be called a house of prayer for people of all nations'), would have upset many, and scared the Jewish authorities (and probably the Romans as well) as this was a highly subversive act. Many might have thought that Jesus was about to stage an uprising. Zealot sympathisers might have started to abandon him when they saw that this incident was not meant to lead to armed revolt.

According to Luke 21:6 Jesus once declared that the stones of the Temple would be torn down. Considering how careful the Jews were to avoid blasphemy against the Temple, these actions and words must have been shocking.

The Western Wall. 'All this you see – the time will come when not a single stone here will be left in place; every one will be thown down.'

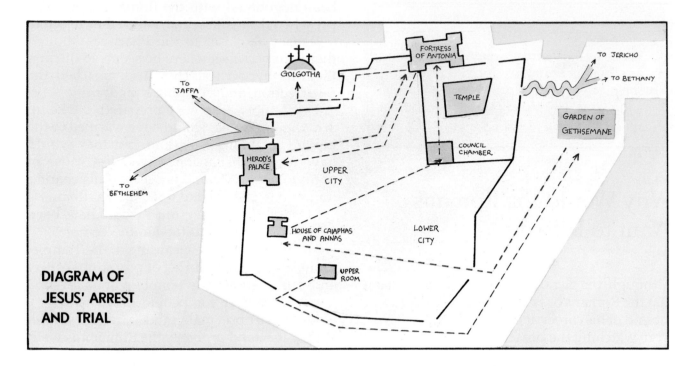

DIAGRAM OF JESUS' ARREST AND TRIAL

The Jewish Trial

Jesus was taken first to the house of Annas, the father-in-law of Caiaphas (he had been High Priest himself until recently, and was still seen as a sort of honorary High Priest). Annas questioned Jesus and then sent him to Caiaphas, who assembled as many of the Sanhedrin as he could in the middle of the night (see Mark 14:53–65).

At daybreak, Jesus was taken before the full Sanhedrin so they could approve the sentence passed (see Luke 22:66–71).

Jesus was then sent to Pilate, to Herod, and back to Pilate again.

Jesus would have left the Upper Room at about 9.00p.m. on Thursday and would have been put on a cross about 9.00a.m. on Friday.

The Synoptic Gospels claim that a charge of blasphemy was brought against Jesus . Mark's Gospel states that Jesus admitted he was the Son of Man who was to come in glory. This is strange, for claiming to be the Messiah was not blasphemous. Luke makes no mention of the attitude shown to the Temple (Matthew 26:61; Mark 15:58), which is surprising, as slandering the Temple was considered to be blasphemous.

Stories of Conflict

The Sadducees – Questions about the Resurrection
(Matthew 22:23–33; Mark 12:18–27; Luke 20:27–40)

The Sadducees once questioned Jesus about the resurrection. They quoted the Law of Moses that provided for a man to marry his dead brother's wife to raise heirs for the dead brother's name. They told a story about seven brothers. The first married, and then died,the second took her as a wife and then died. This kept on happening until all seven died. They posed the question, 'Now, on the day the dead rise to life,whose wife will she be? All seven of them had married her? ' (Luke 20:33)

Jesus replied that the people of the age to come would not marry; 'They will be like the angels and cannot die.' He also pointed out that God had spoken to Moses as 'the God of Abraham, Isaac, and Jacob', suggesting that they were alive with him. 'He is the God of the living, not of the dead, for to him all are alive.'(v38)

The Pharisees

The Sabbath
(Matthew 9:14–17; Mark 2:18–22; Luke 5:33–9)

SCANDAL!
JESUS BREAKS THE SABBATH!

Jesus often challenged traditions that the Pharisees followed. They followed oral tradition, as well as, the written Torah. Jesus seemed to dismiss these, but he offered radical interpretations of the Torah. Mercy and compassion were the most important rules for Jesus, and other Torah laws could be set aside in special circumstances if it was the most loving thing to do.

For example, the Sabbath, was the day of rest from all work, so the Pharisees objected to Jesus' disciples picking ears of corn. Jesus reminded them of the action of King David – once, David and his men had eaten the sacred bread in the Holy Place that should only have been eaten by the priests. He was compassionate as they were starving. Jesus ended by saying; ' "The Sabbath was made for the good of man; man was not made for the Sabbath. So, the Son of Man is Lord even of the Sabbath." ' (Mark 2:27–8)

The same theme is found when Jesus was challenged about healing on the Sabbath (e.g. the healing of the man with a paralysed hand, Matthew12:9–14; Mark 3:1–6; Luke 6:6–11).

Jesus points out that the Torah allows someone to help a wounded or trapped animal on the Sabbath, so why not a human being? ' "What does our Law allow us to do on the Sabbath? To help or to harm? To save a man's life or to destroy it?" ' (Mark 3:4)

The Jewish Sabbath is still celebrated from sunset on Friday until Saturday evening. This begins with a meal on the Friday, when families gather. Bread and wine are blessed and shared, along with a meal.

Christians changed their Sabbath to a Sunday because this was the day Jesus rose again. Christians differ in how strictly they keep the Sabbath. While many were strict in the past,

A Jewish Sabbath meal.

attitudes are more relaxed now. Some have to do shift-work on Sundays, and most are happy to play sports or engage in leisure activities. Some will not buy or sell anything, while most are happy to buy a meal, petrol or various items. The important thing is to meet for worship on that day, and to have a good rest.

This is actor, Ian Charleston, playing champion runner Eric Liddel in the film *Chariots of Fire*. This tells the story of how Liddel refused to run on the Sabbath because he was a committed Christian.

Eating with Sinners
(Luke 7:36–50)

Luke relates the time when Jesus was invited to the home of a Pharisee, Simon. A prostitute entered and wept at Jesus' feet, wiping his feet with her hair. This caused a scandal, and Simon said to himself; ' "If this man really were a prophet, he would know who this woman is who is touching him; he would know what kind of sinful life she lives" !'

Jesus told a parable about two people who owed money. One owed 500 silver coins, and one 50. Both debts were cancelled by the money-lender.

WHICH ONE, THEN, WILL LOVE HIM MORE?

Simon replied that it was the one who was forgiven more. Jesus quickly pointed out that it was like this with the woman. She had been forgiven a great deal. He also gently rebuked Simon for not providing water for his feet (a common custom in the East where it was dusty and sandy), but the woman had cleaned his feet with her tears.

This incident is typical of Jesus' attitude to the outsiders of the day, the prostitues, the tax-collectors, the lepers. He preached a God of mercy who would invite everyone into his Kingdom, and often, it would be the outcasts who got in first, because they knew how great their needs were.

This offended the Pharisees who were very strict about keeping the Torah, and chose not to mix so readily with 'sinners'.

Authority to Forgive Sins
(Mark 2:1–12)

The story of the healing of the paralysed man who was lowered through the roof (see p.99) caused offence because Jesus told the man his sins were forgiven. Some teachers of the Law said, 'How does he dare talk like this? This is blasphemy! God is the only one who can forgive sins!' (v7)

This is also found in the story of the woman in Simon's house. Jesus tells her that her sins are forgiven. Pharisees at the table ask, 'Who is this, who even forgives sins?' Rabbis or holy men might pray that God **would** forgive, but to declare that God **had** forgiven was something much more daring. Christians see this as stemming from his authority as Messiah, or as God incarnate.

The Temple Tax
(Matthew 22:15–22; Mark 12:13–17; Luke 20:20–6)

The Jews at the time of Jesus had to pay two taxes, one to Rome and one to the Temple. The Pharisees believd in paying the latter, and the Herodians the former. Together they challenged Jesus by asking him his opinion on paying taxes. His response disarmed both of them; he picked up a coin and pointed to the head of the Emperor on it. 'Well, then, pay the Emperor what belongs to the Emperor, and pay God what belongs to God.' This meant pay both taxes, to Rome and the Temple.

It can be argued that this was fair, as Rome brought its culture and administration to Judaea, and the Temple was to be honoured as a holy place. The question that Jesus was asked, however, was loaded. It was highly sensitive and political.

The 'Zealot' sympathisers were against paying to Caesar as this reminded them of their lack of independence. The Pharisees had refused to support Herod Archelaus as king, and invited

Roman rule. The Herodians compromised on religious matters – Herod ruled so long as he allowed Roman temples in the land.

It is difficult to draw clear ideas about Christian involvement in politics from this incident.

The Tax Collector
(Luke 19:1–10)

Luke relates the story of a tax collector, Zacchaeus. He would have been immensely unpopular with the people as he worked for the Romans and cheated the people out of their taxes. He was curious to see who Jesus was, and climbed a sycamore tree to get a better view because he was short. Jesus saw him and invited himself to his house! Moved by Jesus' compassion, Zacchaeus vowed to pay back fourfold those he had cheated. This was based upon Exodus 22:1 in the Torah; 'If a man steals a cow or a sheep and kills it or sells it, he must pay five cows for one cow, and four sheep for one sheep.' Jesus declared, 'Salvation has come to this house today,' (v9).

Jesus' attitude to Zacchaeus was typical of his compassion for social outcasts and his understanding of what people were on the inside.

How to be a Disciple
(Luke 10:38–42)

Luke relates the incident in the home of Mary and Martha followers of Jesus. Mary sits at his feet and listens to his teaching, as Martha hurries about the house. She complains that Jesus is not urging Mary to help her. Jesus replies, ' "You are worried and troubled over so many things, but just one is needed. Mary has chosen the right thing, and it will not be taken away from her." ' (v41)

Christians see the importance of prayer and meditation in this story. They feel the need to be quiet, to pray, to feel the presence of God, and to study the Bible to gain inner strength.

Helping a Gentile Woman
(Matthew 15:21–8; Mark 7:24–30)

Jesus was approached by a Phoenicean woman from Tyre. She begged him to help her daughter, who was troubled by an evil spirit. Jesus showed surprise that a Gentile (a non-Jew) had approached him. Jesus tested her by saying, 'Let us first feed the children. It isn't right to take the children's food and throw it to the dogs.' (Gentiles were sometimes called 'dogs' to emphasise that they were outside the covenant with God.) She replied, 'Sir...even the dogs under the table eat the children's leftovers!'

Jesus praised her faith and determination, and said it was greater than the faith he had found in Israel. She went home to find her daughter healed.

While the Hebrew Bible made it clear that Israel were God's chosen people, other nations were also under God's care. Israel was chosen to teach others the way of the one God. (See Isaiah 49:6; 'I will also make you a light to the nations so that all the world may be saved.') At the time of Jesus, some had began to think that others were cursed and outside the mercy of God. Jesus' action was a reminder of the true vocation of Israel to be 'a light to the nations'.

Activities

Key Elements

1 List the different groups who opposed Jesus.

2 How did the Sadducees try to trap Jesus by their parable? How did Jesus answer them?

3 List four things that offended the Pharisees.

4 Why did Jesus cause offence on the Sabbath? How did he reply to criticism?

5 What taxes the Jews had to pay?

6 How did Jesus reply to the question about taxes, and what was he trying to say?

7 Who was Zacchaeus?

8 Why did Jesus' eating with Zacchaeus cause offence?

9 What happened in Mary and Martha's house?

10 What happened near the city of Tyre?

11 Why would the story of the Gentile woman approaching Jesus have been so surprising to many at the time?

Think About It

12 Discuss, in groups, 'Who are society's outsiders today?' Write a modern Gospel story using some of these people.

13 Jesus often threatened tradition. What traditions would you like to see challenged in your life, home, school, or nation? What traditions would you not like to have challenged?

War and Peace

Christians have different points of view about fighting in wars. From the conflict stories in the Gospels, Jesus seems to have followed a non-violent approach.

▶ Jesus avoided confrontation when asked about paying taxes. His reply was clever and made the questioners think. He did not side with those who opposed Rome, or those who worked with Rome.

▶ Jesus was not afraid to stand up to traditions that he felt were a burden and against the mercy of God. He was obviously very brave, and faced fierce criticism without threatening those who opposed him.

▶ Jesus was quiet before Pilate. He did not plead for his life, or insult the procurator. He went to the cross rather than allow his disciples to fight to save him.

▶ At his arrest in the Garden of Gethsemane, Jesus told Peter, 'All who take the sword will die by the sword.'

▶ In the Sermon on the Mount, Jesus told people to turn the other cheek, if they were slapped in the face, and to pray for their enemies.

On the other hand, Jesus went into the Temple and overturned the tables of the money-changers. John's Gospel even says that he took a whip to drive them out! (John 2:15)

Some use this incident as a pretext for using violence when they believe the cause is just. Others point out that it does not say that Jesus actually hurt anyone when he did this, and a limited use of force is not like warfare, where people are killed.

The early Christians seem to have been pacifists (refusing to use violence) and would not take up military service except for police duties. Later, the Church agreed that Christians could fight in wars so long as it was in a just cause. Thomas Aquinas worked out a set of rules for this in the thirteenth century CE:

1 The war must be started by a ruler or government with proper authority.
2 There must be a just cause.
3 The aim of fighting is to right a wrong.
4 Civilians should not be involved in the fighting.
5 Proportionality must be used, meaning that undue force should not be used to defeat the enemy.

This is called the 'Just War' theory.

In modern warfare it is difficult to comply with point 4. Even if only military targets are bombed, civilian workers are likely to be killed. These rules still guide many believers in making up their mind whether to fight in a war. Other believers are pacifists.

I AM A CHRISTIAN, AND I FEEL I HAVE A DUTY TO DEFEND MY NATION FROM PEOPLE WHO WOULD ATTACK US.

I AM A CHRISTIAN, AND BECAUSE OF THIS I JUST CANNOT FIGHT. I FOLLOW THE PRINCE OF PEACE.

Discuss

* Discuss in groups the responses of the people in the picture. Work out questions to ask them.

The story of Ken Lancaster

Ken was orphaned, and was brought up by foster parents who were violent towards him. He became violent himself, involved in burglary by the age of 10. He ran away from home at 13, and punched a policeman in the jaw, knocking him unconscious. He became a minder with gangsters and spent 12 years in prison, but tried to go straight once moving to Sussex. This did not last, and his wife left him.

During his final time in prison he was approached to do a job once he was released. He was offered a few thousand pounds if he would kill someone, and he was given a gun.

He said he would do it, but with his fists only – he did not use weapons.

The turning point came one Christmas when he was staring out at the night sky, looking at the many stars. A profound experience of the reality of God overwhelmed him, and he heard an inner voice saying a verse from Psalm 23; 'he restores my soul'. He was crying – something he had not done for years. When his cellmates came back into the cell, he could not stand them swearing.

He knew he could not kill the man, and so he refused the job. His wife wrote to him out of the blue inviting him to return once he got out.

Ken started going to Church, and changed his ways. A power had come upon him, met him, and turned him round. He has gone straight ever since, though he has had to struggle not to thump some when they upset him, for that was the way he lived for so long!

Ken, as an ex-convict, is the sort of person who might find himself a social outcast, mistrusted and not given new opportunities. However, he has found love, forgiveness and acceptance through his new faith in Jesus.

Activity

* Imagine that you are Ken. Write a letter to your wife after your conversion, saying how different you feel.

Vocabulary

Sabbath   prostitute
Gentile   'Just War'

Revision Questions

1 a) State four different kinds of power shown by Jesus in the miracle stories. Give an example for each one.
b) Explain which other parts of the Gospel accounts portray Jesus as a special person.
c) Do you think the miracles of Jesus are more important than the teaching of Jesus? Give reasons to support your opinion.

2 a) Give an outline of the conversation between Jesus and the devil when Jesus was tempted in the wilderness.
b) Give an outline of the conversation between Jesus and Peter at Caesarea Philippi to where Peter called Jesus 'the Christ' (Messiah).
c) Explain, why, soon afterwards, Jesus said to Peter, 'Out of my sight, Satan.'
d) Explain how the teaching Jesus gave at Ceasarea Philippi would help his followers when they faced persecution and the temptation to deny him.
e) (i) How far do you think Christians today face the same temptations as the first followers did?
(ii) Do you think it is easier or harder for Christians to face temptations today? Give reasons.

3 a) Write an account of the parable of the sheep and the goats and state what it teaches about the Kingdom of God.
b) Give an account of any one other parable about the Kingdom of God and state the meaning.
c) Explain briefly what other teachings there are in the Synoptic Gospels about the Kingdom of God, besides the two parables you have given.
d) If Jesus brought the Kingdom of God, why do you think the world is in the state it is today?

4 a) Luke says that Jesus told the parables of the Lost Sheep, Lost Coin and Lost Son because 'the Pharisees and the Scribes murmured'. What were they complaining about?
b) How does Jesus answer their complaint in the parable of the Lost Coin?
c) How does the elder brother in the parable of the Lost Son behave like the Pharisees and the Scribes?
d) Jesus preached forgiveness; he also showed forgiveness in the way he behaved. What evidence is there in the Gospels to support this?
e) 'God is so loving he will forgive everybody.' How far do you think this is true to what Jesus taught about God? Give evidence from the teaching of Jesus.

5 a) Jesus said to his disciples, 'All of you will run away and leave me.' (Mark 14:27) What did Jesus and Peter say to each other during the Last Supper.
b) What happened that same night? (Show how Jesus' prediction came true.)
c) Explain how Jesus showed courage and self-control during his arrest and trials.
d) What suggests that Pilate did not want Jesus to be executed? What do you think of his motives?

1

The Birth of Christ.

Read Matthew 1:18–25
  a) How does the Gospel writer show that Joseph was a 'good' man?
  b) Explain fully what the writer of the Gospel believes about Jesus in the above passage.
  c) 'You can't be a Christian if you don't believe this story!' Would you agree with this point of view?
  d) In the picture above, are any details not present in the account in Matthew? Where else might you read about these?

2

Baptism of Christ by Francesco Albani.

a) What is the bird in this picture?
b) Explain what the bird symbolises.
c) How do the Evangelists link John the Baptist with Elijah?
d) In what other way is Jesus shown to be special in this story?
e) Do you think Jesus needed to be baptised? Give reasons for your answer.

3

a) Write a brief account of the event shown in the picture.
b) Explain the importance of this event:
   (i) for Jesus
   (ii) for Christians today.
c) Jesus was misunderstood then and people misunderstand him today. Do you agree? Give reasons for your answer.

4

a) Who is the disciple being helped by Jesus?
b) Why was this man sinking?
c) What does this story tell Christians about Jesus?
d) What other story was told about a stormy sea and Jesus?
e) Why do you think these stories were important for the early Christians?
f) Do you think it is important to know if these stories actually happened? Give reasons for your answer.

5

a) An actor is playing the part of Jesus in the above picture. What is happening?
b) How do some Christians remember this event on Good Friday?
c) Why do you think this happened? Give reasons for your answer.
d) List the main characters in the Passion story that you would want to include in a drama sketch based upon it.
e) Which scene would you make the most important and why?

Word List

Annunciation – from the Latin 'to announce'. The greeting and message given to Mary by the angel Gabriel, telling her she had been chosen to give birth to Jesus.

Baptism – ritual of water pouring, or immersion, in the name of the Father, Son and Holy Spirit to show a turning away from an old life.

Bar Mitzvah – 'Son of the Commandment'. A special ceremony is held to mark the occasion when a Jewish boy is 13 years old. He becomes an adult in the affairs of relgion.

Base communities – local churces formed in the poorer areas of cities in Latin America. Ordinary people are trained as teachers and co-ordinators.

Beatitudes – the short sayings of Jesus from the Sermon on the Mount about who is happy and blessed.

Circumcision – the removal of the foreskin of the penis. This is used in Judaism as a sign of the covenant, of being set apart for God.

Covenant – a special agreement or promise in the Bible. It is a special relationship between God and Israel in the Old Testament, and the Church in the New Testament.

Creed – from the word 'credo', 'I believe'. A statement of beliefs.

Disciple – learner, student or follower.

Dunamis – a Greek word which is similar to the words 'dynamo' or 'dynamite'. It is used to describe the power of the Holy Spirit.

Easter – the celebration of the death and resurrection of Jesus.

Essene – a member of a Jewish monastic group at the time of Jesus.

Eucharist – 'thanksgiving' meal; the Communion of bread and wine remembering the death and resurrection of Jesus. (Also called Mass, Lord's Supper, Holy Communion and Breaking of Bread.)

Evangelion – Greek word on which the word Gospel 'good news' is based.

Evangelist – writer of a Gospel.

Exorcism – casting out of evil spirits.

Gentile – anyone who is not a Jew.

Good Friday – the day when the death of Jesus is particularly remembered.

Gospel – 'good news' book, telling about the life of Jesus.

Holy Place – the holiest part of the Temple in Jerusalem where only the High Priest could go.

Hosanna – a Hebrew word meaning 'save us' or 'set us free'.

Kingdom of God – the reign of God; a time of peace and blessing.

Just War – the belief that some wars may be fought if there is a just cause for doing so.

'L' – material only found in Luke's Gospel.

Levite – and assistant and server in the Temple.

Liberation Theology – developed in South America. The teaching that beliefs about God should set people free. This may happen through political action.

'M' – material only found in Matthew's Gospel.

Magnificat – Mary's song after receiving the news about Jesus from the angel Gabriel.

Messiah – 'anointed one', believed to be a special person set apart for God bringing freedom from oppression and peace on earth.

Messianic Jews – Jews who believe that the Messiah has come in the person of Jesus.

Miracle – event which cannot be explained scientifically but which is seen as having religious significance.

Nunc Dimittis – Simeon's song of thanks after he had seen Jesus being presented in the Temple.

Parable – a story with a moral.

Parousia – the return of Christ in glory.

Passover – Jewish festival remembering the exodus from Egypt.

Pentecost – Jewish festival, also when the Holy Spirit was given to the disciples.

Pharisees – a Jewish party, believing in many oral traditions as well as the written Torah.

'Q' – 'quelle' German for 'source'. Material found in both Matthew and Luke.

Rabbi – a Jewish teacher of the Torah.

Resurrection – rising from the dead in a new, transformed body.

Sabbath – day of rest from Friday p.m. to Saturday p.m.

Sadducees – Jewish ruling party, only believing in the Torah as Scripture.

Samaritans – inhabitants of Samaria. These people were not descended from the ancient Hebrews.

Shekinah – the presence of the Holy Spirit.

Synoptics – the Gospels of Matthew, Mark and Luke.

Tabernacle – the sacred tent, used in the days when the Hebrews lived in the desert.

Tefillin – phylacteries; boxes with leather straps that are attached to the head and the left arm. They contain portions of the Torah.

Theotokos – 'God bearer', a name given to Mary by some Christians because she carried God (Jesus) in her womb.

Transfiguration – where Jesus' appearance altered and shone with light.

Transignification – where the bread and wine of Communion convey Jesus to the worshippers. They take on a new significance, representing Jesus' body and blood.

Transubstantiation – where the bread and the wine are transformed into the body and blood of Jesus, but still appear as bread and wine on the outside.

Torah – the Law of Moses, being the first five books of the Hebrew Bible.

Zealots – a Jewish group who were prepared to use terrorist actions to drive out the Romans.

Index